Aela's Story

Aela's Story

M. Dumonceaux

AELA'S STORY

iUniverse books may be ordered through booksellers or by contacting:

iUniverse
1663 Liberty Drive
Bloomington, IN 47403
www.iuniverse.com
1-800-Authors (1-800-288-4677)

Because of the dynamic nature of the Internet, any web addresses or links contained in this book may have changed since publication and may no longer be valid. The views expressed in this work are solely those of the author and do not necessarily reflect the views of the publisher, and the publisher hereby disclaims any responsibility for them.

ISBN: 978-1-5320-6083-0 (sc)
ISBN: 978-1-5320-6085-4 (hc)
ISBN: 978-1-5320-6084-7 (e)

Library of Congress Control Number: 2018914909

Print information available on the last page.

iUniverse rev. date: 01/14/2019

Part 1

Chapter 1

S omething happens as I touch the flowers. The blooms, which are white, turn deep red instantly as I hold them. Like a flash of light in my head, I know that my world is changing.

Such a sickness washes over me, pounding and roaring in my head, and I feel like I'm falling backward even as I drop forward, facedown into the ground. I hear screams, sobbing, and horrible sounds, yet when my eyes open, I see only leaves and damp earth. Something is so wrong.

I lie there for a long time on the forest floor, listening to sounds that I know are only in my head. I open my hand and see that the crushed flowers are white again, but the stains they have left on my skin are red.

After a while, the noises fade. I know I must get up and find the meaning of such an omen.

How can I? I am so weak and unwilling. Please do not make me.

I gather the plants that spilled from my arms when I fell. I am shaking; I cannot think straight, but still, I know they must not be wasted. I might need them in the days to come.

I fold the white flowers in a scrap of fabric, shuddering, and push them to the bottom of my bag. I scrub at the stain on my hand with the hem of my skirt, but it will not come off. The flowers hold a power that I do not understand but will have to learn. All I can know is that it rules me and not I it.

There is no need to run; instinctively, I know this too. I walk.

I go into woods that, for the first time, feel hostile—a world that resents my presence now at this moment. What sanctuary it offers is not for me.

I try to reason with myself. I try to lie to myself.

Perhaps my mind only goes where it has been led by stories told breathlessly in fields and great halls—stories made so much worse by knowing they all end the same way.

Perhaps even now the tables are being set and the ale poured for the evening meal.

I know what I will find when I come to the edge of the village. But knowing and seeing are two vastly different things. My first lesson is looking upon the silent leavings of all that I know and love.

The dead hushed in absolute stillness. The wind has left.

Such horrible, hateful silence. Death lies in the shadows, looking out at me, everywhere at once—quietly, boldly, triumphantly.

The hall has not been torched, nor have any of the houses. Frozen sick as I am, I know it was not mercy that kept raiders' hands from firing the roof thatch. They have hopes of coming back to occupy the village as winter draws near and river ice steals the fierce from their longships. Any fool can know this.

But that such a thing can be! Bloody, murderous hands and evil spirits here in my father's village. At home here. I would sooner die than see something like that.

I force myself to walk through, speaking the names aloud as I find them, calling them out to the birds, the absent winds, and all the witnesses of the wild woods around.

The names of those who lie still on the ground and those who are missing.

When I know them all, I stand rigid in the twilight, feeling them burn themselves into my heart and taking their places in my memory, ready to be carried with me.

Only then do I turn toward the great hall, where I know I will find my family.

Do I sound strong? Fierce and loyal?

Not in this world.

My father will have fought like the very fiends to save his family, to his last breath.

So it is. He lies not far from the door, twisted down into death, where he has fallen.

He was a strong warrior, and it took many blows to overcome him. I count them—a number to hate, to thwart.

His blood soaks the ground beneath him, giving itself to the earth.

What can I say here?

To put words to that kind of pain is to relive it. Forever. I will not.

My legs give way beneath me, and I crumple to the ground beside him. I lay my hands on his head and hope the pain will kill me. It is the most private pain, here inside me; no one will ever know it.

Then words come anyway, unwanted as they are.

How can it be that his spirit is gone? How can I endure being awake and aware today and tomorrow and all the rest of my days without him?

I scream at the sky. I scream to drown the words, and twist and sob, digging my nails into my arms and shredding my skin. I hate harder than I ever knew I could. I hate what has happened. I hate that I had no say in it. That I cannot change it.

I hate the person I will now have to be. I mourn for my father and myself.

I try for hours to cry myself to death, through the darkness of night and into oblivion. At length, exhausted, I sleep.

I open my eyes to find scavengers feasting in the silent gray dawn. Bloodied beaks and talons taking their due. A raven looking at me with his living eye, both of us knowing where this game will end.

I jump to my feet, shouting and waving my arms to send them flying. Then I am screaming wildly and running, trying to catch them and make someone or something pay. I run and lose over and over again until I run out of breath.

They will be back. I cannot stop them alone, but they will never tear at my father's flesh; this I can do.

I have loved my father like no other person on earth. It never entered my mind that one day he might be taken from me, simply because my mind could not conceive of it.

How heavy he is in death. It takes all my strength to drag him into the hall.

There, I find my mother.

One arm wrapped around her dog, as if she could save him from the axe that killed both of them. At least they did not use her first. Too old for the markets, she was left to bleed her life into the floor of the hall that had sheltered her.

A shiver and a new hatred.

I bring my father's body close to my mother's. I lay their limbs straight. I find blankets to cover the desecration. I comb their hair and wash their faces. Gently, I lay the faithful dog between them. I make them mine again.

I kiss my father's fingertips and then his forehead. It is the hardest thing I have ever done.

I stand in the shadows of the hall, feeling the silence like winter on my skin.

Feeling defeated and overwhelmed. So helpless.

Everything inside me is bruised. It hurts to think and to move.

How does such a thing happen?

I go to the hearth, where I find scattered ash and pots strewn about, bones and pieces of meat, broken beakers, and more death. Raiders who had no mercy to spare for the elders, and none for the babies. What kind of men are these? What kind of animals?

I stand, weak and weeping, for the lost lives of our family, for the bloodlines that ended there at my feet.

Then it comes to me, creeping out at the worst possible moment from its hiding place at the back of my mind—knowledge I do not want, knowledge that comes like a blow to my head.

Violating me, teaching me like death never could.

I feel that same sick feeling where your heart pounds through your senses and tries to drown itself. Already I know it so well, the feeling that your world has gone mad. Your legs buckle, and your bones melt.

It beats you down until there is nothing left but to know.

I do not find my sister, Ymma. She is not here.

It is so much. Too much. Way beyond what I can handle.

I scream and howl as if I can vanquish the silence and the deed together. Screaming out my hate, my fear, and my horrible knowing. Again.

Bad enough if she were dead, it is far worse that she is among the missing.

My lovely, gentle sister, with her soft hands and warm heart, being carried away to be sold in the markets like an animal. By animals.

No. Don't think it. Push it away.

After that, I begin to work, doing the things I can, without thinking or feeling.

I have no idea how long—hours.

I gather what food I can find and warm clothing. I find two small daggers, rope, my mother's medicinal herbs, and her cup of carved bone. I take the small hoard of gold and silver pieces the raiders missed, hidden beneath the hearthstones. I do not care about such a thing at such a time, but I take them.

At last, I stand before my tapestry, looking at the work I have been doing: a tree, twined and intricate. My father's family, himself the strong upright trunk, embracing branches of loved ones.

It is a slap to the face.

I want to tear it from its frame and rip it to shreds with my teeth.

4

It is a lie the gods have told. To our faces. Shamelessly.

With fingers that feel nothing, I carefully undo the threads that hold it, roll it up tightly and tie it around my waist, under my tunic.

It is something else to push away.

The sun is high by this time. I kneel before the hearth, where I have collected leaves and kindling, and soon I have built a good fire.

My bag and bundle lie by the door, and I stand in the center of the great hall, bidding goodbye with my eyes, my heart, and my skin.

Then I take a torch and stand on tables and beds, lighting the dry roof thatch where I can reach it.

Carefully, I light the circle of wood that surrounds my parents.

When I know it will burn, I walk out of the hall and into my cold new world.

Then I fire the roofs and haystacks of the village, calling all the names again, remembering all that I know of them and memorizing them the way they want to be remembered.

One by one, I light the funeral pyres, lighting the way.

I stand, watching the cleansing flames as they claim my people and then link themselves together and share their strength.

Soon the fire heaves, massive, into the sky and forces me into the cool of the woods.

I lean on the tree behind me and let myself be blinded by pain.

And now there is noise, a great rushing of wind, as if all the spirits are swept away at once into the smoke and sky.

I feel it then—how alone I am.

Chapter 2

Again, the sun is forcing me awake. I must have slipped to the ground and slept through the night into dawn. I close my eyes and turn my face into my arm, as if I have strength to fight the brutal assault of awareness.

Then I freeze. I hear voices—men moving around and calling to one another. I hold my breath. I count to thirteen. I keep still, listening. I feel sweet relief when I understand them. They are not Northmen, not death-bringing beasts.

They are good men, speaking good Saxon. When I rise to my feet, the man standing closest to me turns quickly, sword in hand. Then he sees me, sheathes his weapon, and shouts to the others, who come running.

They gather around me, talking excitedly all at once so that I do not know whom to answer or how. Their leader raises his hand.

"Silence! She cannot answer if we overwhelm her with noise." He turns to me. "Girl, are you the only one left then?"

I raise my chin until my eyes look fully into his. I nod. He shivers.

"When did this happen? How is it that they did not take you?"

I tell them I was gathering in the woods, far from home, and returned to find the village—my village—full of soulless faces and nothing else, with no one to hold accountable.

I tell them that my father was lord of this place and that it is I who torched the hall and village. I watch it light again in their eyes.

Their leader speaks with the carefully calm voice of reason and safety.

"I am Hengest. We saw the light in the night sky and guessed that raiders had struck. We came to see if we might help, but I knew we would be too late." One and all, they bristle, taller and harder, ready to fight and half-lit themselves. It is my turn to shiver.

These are frustrated men growing restless now and eager to be away.

"It was good that we came, for you would not survive long alone in these woods. Come with us to our village." He looks back to the smoldering ruins. "There is nothing to look for? It is their way to leave little behind but carrion."

I shake my head; hold up my bundle, all my life in an armful; and walk with them to their horses. I am so cold. I feel as if I will never be warm again.

I sit in front of a warrior who tells me his name and says that I may sleep if I need to and his arms will keep me from falling.

Then he begins to talk of his family and the people who live in his village. He talks on and on, forcing my mind to make the pictures, when all I want is to give way to the blackness of despair.

I know he means well, but I hate him for it, growing ever more rigid and tense through the long ride to their village. Will he never stop?

Still, by the time the moon lights the forest around us, I slump against his shoulder in sleep. The sudden noise of the villagers and the light of the fires beyond make me start with fear.

Arms come at me in the dimness, women taking charge of me and pushing the men away.

They lead me to a fire, where I drink ale and eat meat until I feel sick. Beside me sits the village healer, Gytha, who says, "It will be long since you have eaten. Stop now so you do not give it all back."

I look at her face while I wipe mine, reading the lines and finding the eyes.

I try to smile. I cannot. I curl myself down onto the ground, wrap my cloak around me, and watch the flames dance with the night sky. Gytha washes my hands for me as if I am a child. Then she pulls my head to her lap and strokes my hair, coaxing bits of leaves free from the tangles. Eventually, I sleep.

She makes a space for me in her hut. I speak little, sitting on the floor beside the fire and watching her as she does her work. She is silent as she sorts plants and seeds carefully, but when she prepares food, she tells me about the village and its people.

She has been alive for so long she can remember a time when the land was free from the raids of the Northmen. As a child, she ran in the woods with her sister. They were twins who could not be told apart, even by their mother, and they never feared.

She has outlived her children: a daughter lost to milk fever, and the grandchild with her, and a son who lived long but was childless. Of her

7

twin she never speaks, save once, when she tells me her name, Saegyth, and then tells me never to say it and to forget I heard it.

She need not have worried; I say nothing to anyone for a long time.

She is the midwife for the area, as well as the healer. Sick things come to her, man and animal alike, and when she can, she makes them well. When she cannot, she takes them in, into her hut and under her care, until they breathe their last.

It takes me a while to realize this, and once I understand, I run from the hut, angry and shaking. If a decision like that has to be made, it will never be hers or anyone else's, just mine.

She finds me in the woods. I keep my face turned from her so she will know I am not hers. She could have laughed or scorned such a childish thing, but she comes close instead and speaks with a soft voice that calms me instantly.

"You are not the same as the others I care for," she says. "I have known you would come since before you were born." Then she pulls her tunic down from the shoulder until the skin shows white where it has not seen the sun for years. I look and see the same pattern of red stain that remains on my hand from the strange white blooms.

"I picked an unusual white flower myself, Aela. The only one I have ever seen in my life," she says. "I found it by a spring in the woods, and as I first saw it, a wave of sorrow rang sharp through me.

"I fell to the ground, and a dream came to me of great terror and evil, with the world awash in flames and blood. Then the wind came and blew it all away, and where the flames had raged, there lay a small baby girl with dark hair and white skin."

Past and pain chase themselves across her face. "I thought the prophecy fulfilled when I gave birth to my beautiful daughter. The gods showed me soon enough the truth of it."

She takes my hand and smooths the red marks on my palm with her fingertips. Then she places my hand to cover the marks on her shoulder, they are exactly the same. "When I awoke from my dream, I was lying on my back, and the bloom lay here on my heart."

Tears fall silently down my face. I do not understand what binds us together, but I cannot deny it, and the gods know I need it.

"When the raiders destroyed your people, I felt them. I felt the evil course through me, and the red blooms on my breast were seared with pain. I wept for you, and I waited. I knew that you would come to me from loss and horror and that I would help you to raise your head to the sky again. Let me, Aela."

She frames my face with her hands and presses her lips to my forehead. They are the hands of a healer and the lips of a mother. She speaks the words of a bard.

She is not strong, but she pulls me to my feet and holds me up through the long walk back to the village. After that, I am willing to remain in her hut, keeping the fire lit, helping her make poultices, and pounding herbs.

The people look on me kindly and speak in hushed voices when I am near. Although I tend their wounds and nurse their children, they know me to be still a sick thing myself, so they accept my silence and my seclusion.

The days I can deal with, one at a time and filled with work, but the nights I dread. I run from choking sleeplessness in the darkness of the hut into the forest, as far as it takes to feel alone. By turns, I rage like a madwoman or wail my sorrow into the black skies and the cold earth.

In truth, I am never alone; always someone watches from the darkness. Gytha takes no chances that I will somehow be taken from her; she knows more than most about the fates, and they cannot be trusted.

By winter's end, I know the names of all the women in the village and most of the rest.

I still cannot think of my family, while I silently grieve for them. They remain away with all the other things I cannot allow myself to remember— or forget.

9

Chapter 3

I want to become a midwife. Gytha talks endlessly about what is required of one.

"Birthing is a fearsome and mysterious thing," she says. "An ordeal that women must endure alone."

Not for them the strength of martial kinship, nor the training, weapons, armor, and careful preparation. Not for them either the glory in the battle; or the songs sung in the firelight. Instead, each birth must be faced as a price to be paid—the tribute demanded by love and lust and the ransom for the future.

She smiles without her eyes. "It is how I know that the gods favor men. It costs a man nothing to see himself in the face of another, but a woman pays dearly. Such a rigorous test is a way to ensure that only the strongest live on."

She builds with her words an army of women warriors, part of an elite fighting force, battle scarred and able to forget swiftly the horrors of the birthing chamber.

I eagerly accept the idea, confident that when my time comes, I will be strong, and my children will survive to carry the lines of my family—my dead family, whose blood still cries out, unavenged, from the earth.

This innocent arrogance lasts only until I attend my first birthing and come face-to-face with the waking nightmare that it is.

We have all heard the screams that come from a woman's hut while she is struggling to deliver her child. You look at one another helplessly with a sick feeling in your belly and useless empathy in your heart.

When the screams last for hours, you try to block them out, and if you are callous or dimwitted, you can shrug it off and scoff at such weakness. But if you listen, if you feel, you come to fear childbirth like nothing else, and if you are a woman who has given birth, the mother's pain will be mirrored in your eyes; you will shiver and send a prayer to the gods.

At sixteen, I am horrified. I carry, and fetch, and help, all the while vowing under my breath never to allow myself to be led to such a pass. I can avenge my family's honor, but the line will live only in song. Words such as *coward* and *weak* are thrust out of my head as soon as they enter. I work on.

Later, when I have learned all that is known of the birthing process—pitifully little, in truth—I ask to be given different duties.

Women have been giving birth for centuries. The earth herself was born of a mother, and for all its mystery and secrets, there are but two endings. I am not a gambler by nature, but I understand the odds of the game. I prefer those of a healer to those of a midwife.

Here I annoy Gytha; I ask far too many questions and am rarely satisfied with the answers.

Is there a better way to spend a winter evening, firelit and close, than looking for truth and sorting out the real from the imagined? What lies are told, and why? Who tells them, and how are they known?

What is the difference between healers and midwives? Why should they not be the same and work the same? A man can come to us with a broken limb or ragged gash, and we will know ways to keep his arm straight and stop blood from flowing. A woman may tear and bleed herself to death in giving birth, and we are almost helpless. No application of herbs and no amount of pressing will stop her blood. Tears in her flesh will heal slowly, if at all.

Is even healing divided up between the winners and the losers, with no system of merit and no reasoning beyond man or woman? Who designs these things?

She who does not heal, whether with the first baby or the fifth, her mind can be numbed so she will not care that she is dying, but she will die, and much of the time, her baby will follow her. Why is it so?

Why do the gods hate women? It goes without saying that they are men. Who else leads in this world?

Why are men to be kept away from the birthing chamber? I answer my own question. They are willing to claim the fruit if they can keep their hands clean. Why is it like this?

I ask other people, men and women, including midwives, and none have an answer that makes sense. All of them look at me as if I am witless.

One day I lose my patience with Gytha's vague replies and shout at her, "Just because something has always been done a certain way does not mean it is the best way or the only way!"

Very disrespectful, I know. I wait for her hand or her voice to free her temper, but she goes quiet, staring at me and slowly growing pale. "Please do not say such things aloud, Aela."

I do not understand how she cannot see such an obvious truth. I try to reason with her.

"Gytha, if men must have some advantage, why should we not do our best to appropriate or, at the very least, exploit it to our advantage? We would be idiots not to. We are idiots. We put up with it. Think about this for a moment. Perhaps a man would see differently than a woman, possibly even indifferently. Enough to think clearly at least. Men's minds might find a change that could be made; they might see better ways to repair damage. They might forge us weapons so we could be less defenseless with our small armory of herbs and linen. No doubt they would enjoy the opportunity to display their natural superiority. Let us by all means encourage them."

Now I have gone too far, and the idea horrifies Gytha. I am slapped on the arm and told to stop talking.

As the dying fire begins to close her face, I can see her mind engaging with it, reluctantly. She is wise for a reason.

Chapter 4

Time passes, and slowly, the wounds in my mind and heart take their shapes. I become familiar with the scars. I count them every so often.

The villagers know me and trust me as they do Gytha to care for their ill, but I remain secluded in our hut most of the time, and that they cannot understand. I see it in their eyes when they come to me; they think, sweetly and sadly, that my mind has been broken. They give me freely that generous, safe leeway given to those who are less.

Endless patience and sympathy, which hurt worse because they are genuine. Others who are less kind say I am weak. How can they know so much yet understand so little?

Of course I am weak. But weak as I am, I am stronger than you, and we both know it. I have survived.

It is suggested that a husband be found for me to relieve the burden carried by Gytha, but we know, the two of us, that I could never be a burden, and we must stay together. So it remains: days of work and nights close together in the circle of firelight, talking.

One of those nights, we hear a kick on our door, and we open it to find a young warrior, or one dressed like it, with a sick face and all the fight gone in him. He cradles a huge hunting dog in his arms like a baby and stands there, cold and mute asking it all with his eyes. Asking if we are daft. Why do we still stand here?

Gytha pulls him in and makes him sit by the hearth. We build up the fire and light every candle we have, but I can tell from her sidelong looks and delaying tactics that Gytha has no hope for the dog.

I raise my brows at her and bend to look closer at the injured animal. He has a huge gash along his side from the front leg back and around to below. Fur has been cut away, and the wound is held shut by strong fingers, white beneath hardened blood. I catch my breath; it is a fearsome wound, and I am surprised the dog is still among us.

"You have been hunting boar, Hemwyth," Gytha says abruptly.

"Yes," he says simply. Just one word. I freeze, as if I really am witless, crouched over the dog in his lap, while the wind whispers down my spine.

Slowly, I bring my eyes up to his face, needing to really see the eyes that go with that voice.

That far-too-deep voice, scratched and almost hostile, beautiful. It just goes straight in like an arrow wound, deep where it counts. Somehow, it connects instantly to something inside me.

His eyes are dark blue and burning with a pain I can understand. I speak the same language. *I will save him for you*, I say with my own eyes, and I try to gently pull his fingers away from the wound. They will not move. I look up at him again and ask, "How long have you been holding him thus?"

"Too long," Gytha says quietly.

Hemwyth jerks and half rises from the stool. "No! He lives yet. See? He breathes!"

It is in neither of us to contradict the warrior we remember he is.

Gytha smiles small and comes to help me work on the wound. Hemwyth's fingers will not loosen.

"Chut! Move your hands. We cannot fix what we cannot see." She squints and draws close to look. I know her eyes betray her in dim light, so I lean her away from him and look closer myself.

"I see well enough," I say, "but still, I would see better. Let us wash both dog and hands to gently remove the cold blood, and then we can look again."

I am not as good with the words as I am with the eyes, apparently.

"But to what end, Aela?" Gytha hisses. "Dogs wounded thus by a boar never return home. They are freed from their pain and left for the ravens. His wound is too ragged and misshapen. Besides, he will have lost much with a wound like that."

"No," Hemwyth says fiercely. "I was there, struggling with the boar, when Gunn came to help me. Other men had come by then also, and when Gunn was raked by the boar's tusks, I shouted to them to take the boar and finish it. I went to Gunn, put what was out back in, and pressed it closed with my hands. I have carried him thus since then, and you must save him. The ravens can wait for their due. He has not died yet, so he will not die."

It is the simple, religious logic of the unenlightened.

14

I listen but keep little; his voice is plucking strings inside me and tangling things. I swing a cauldron of water down from the flames, hoping its heat might claim the flush on my cheeks.

Gytha places her hand on his shoulder. "The gods choose whom they will, man and beast alike, Hemwyth. This you know. Your dog dreams even now of the scraps from their feasting halls."

She fingers our pile of linens absently, her mind working to make lies of her words. "How should I bind such an injury? And how shall the dog be made to keep still while the wound knits itself together? It is impossible."

"I will stitch it closed," I say, as if it is the simplest thing, "and then we will bind it, with a poultice to draw out poisons."

Gytha steps back, surprised and not pleased with my behavior thus far. "What? You will stitch it? You have not stitched a wound yet. Though you have learned much, you will practice new skills on such an injury?"

She shakes her head and pauses. "There. I see it. You know the dog is doomed, and you but wish to learn where opportunity rises. This is sound thinking, Aela, yet I am sorry for the animal and the man who will mourn him. As should you be."

She is wrong. It is her turn to be witless.

She goes to her medicine chest and removes the fine-spun thread and bone needles she uses for stitching gashes.

I have placed our big tub beneath the dog and tested the water for warmth. I scoop out the first bowl and am turning to pour it over the dog's wound, when Hemwyth, never moving his upper half, kicks his leg out and knocks the bowl across the room.

Shocked and soaked, I step back a pace. Witlessness without end.

Before I can thump him—of course, I would not have; he holds the dog—or call him anything, he speaks.

"If you are thinking thus, dark-haired girl, then your eyes have been lying to me. Tell me you will answer for what they have claimed. Show me how you will save him. And do it now. I will hold him."

God in heaven, again that voice. Like music that only I hear. I nod, holding his gaze. I would promise him to make his dog fly.

Thankfully, I do not. I pick up the bowl and begin washing the wound.

"Gytha is mistaken. I do not seek to benefit from such a death. It is true that I have not yet stitched wounds, but I have a good hand with a needle. I have done my tapestry work like any good Thane's daughter, and my eyes are sharp. I will do my best to keep him at your side."

Both of us know the kind of pain his dog will face; neither of us can change it. It is difficult to know who is more afraid.

The slow, gentle motions of cleansing the blood away calm my mind, and before long, I begin to see the lines and shapes of the wound. Carefully moving the strong fingers a hairbreadth at a time to see more clearly, I let them sort themselves out.

Gradually, despite all my senses do to distract me, I begin to see the connections between them and how they might be joined in the most natural way.

It sounds strange to tell it, but lines, shapes, and hollows have always formed pictures in my mind. They arrange themselves in complex pictures and puzzles so that I can see them when they need to be seen.

As it is with frost and tangled leaves, so it is with this flesh, and I can see what stitches are needed and where to form the picture. Having placed Hemwyth's fingers where they do the most good, I take the thread and needle box from Gytha.

She is worried, squeezing my hand anxiously. "He will be angry when you fail," she whispers. "You know that he is the orphaned son of the old lord, a warrior born and through to the core. He is powerful in his own right. Who knows what we may suffer at his hands when the dog dies. Better that you should tell him no. You cannot be blamed for something you have not done."

"Gytha, hush," I say. "There are things about me that even you do not know. I will sew these wounds to the best of my ability, and the gods will judge."

How she does not question that kind of statement from me at a time like this, I can only wonder at.

I sort quickly through the threads, pick the strongest that is yet fine enough for the purpose, and thread the thinnest needle. I am afraid myself but not for my work.

The dog has lain silently this whole time, lost to the waking world. I know my work will rouse him with pain; he will be hard to hold if he struggles, and the fight will likely kill him.

There is nothing else to be done.

I take a deep breath and begin to stitch his wounds, slowly and carefully linking the edges together with straight, simple stiches. On thick fabric, my mind insists. He stays asleep. I could weep with gratitude. I stitch on.

When blood flows, Gytha presses with her cloths, and soon there begins to grow a stark, severe line like long lightning in a heavy sky. Now and then, his muscles twitch and quiver, but the dog sleeps in the safe darkness near death, unmoving and indifferent.

The gods want it that way, so I know him for a favorite.

They keep him in darkness for two days, through stitching and ointment and binding, and all in the arms of Hemwyth, who does not let go. One arm freed long enough to eat the bread and meat that Gytha forces on him and drink some ale, and then the arm is back around his dog.

It is a long time to go without a walk in the woods, but he will yield the dog to none, so we leave him propped in the corner with his face in the shadows.

His dog clearly has the favor of the gods, so I am not consumed with worry, as Hemwyth is. My reassurances fall on deaf ears despite the fact that as far as he and everyone else knows, all healers have influence with the gods.

Instead, I am free to move about the hut—working, cooking, eating, and trying vainly to sleep—in a perfectly normal way, as if he is a patient like any other and as if I am not thoroughly stitched up like the dog, on the end of a line that stops at him.

Like any rope and wand used to draw a circle on the ground, so I will go in a circle around him if I walk forever. He simply takes command of my mind—and my senses and my wits. And why not, since they are undefended?

Two days that feel like a lifetime with hot cheeks and looking away as long as I can stand.

Then, when I might naturally look now and then to see if the dog stirs, I find it too hard to look at him at all. I feel like a fool.

I feel how it is when your mind and your hands are working diligently but the rest of you is somewhere else entirely. I imagine my ear is listening to that heartbeat, my face is buried in his tunic, and I feel his breath on my hair and his hand on my skin.

The whole time I squeeze water from a cloth into the dog's mouth and help to ease it down his throat, my hands are white and my flesh icy, while my blood boils.

It is a good thing I know my work; it is hard enough to hide things from Gytha.

When the time comes to remove his bindings, the dog wakes suddenly and fixes me with his eyes as I cut through the cloth. He watches my face, not my hands, and he does not twitch or move. I slowly pull the cloth free, cutting bits where needed to free it from his fur. The stitches hold firm

17

in their straight lines, while the flesh beneath shows no sign of poison or swelling.

Mess that I am, I still know that such an outcome is a gift to both dog and warrior.

When I look up, I find the man's eyes on my face as well. He holds my gaze as if he owns it, and the dog shifts in his arms, reaches out, and licks my hand.

Chapter 5

G unn stays in our hut for a fortnight; Hemwyth has gone back to the hunt but sends meat for his dog every evening.

Gunn shows his gratitude to the gods by behaving exactly as he must to ensure a good recovery: still at first and beginning to move slowly after a few days.

I never see a dog do such again; not once does he tear at the threads or try to remove them. I know he must be a powerful and fierce hunter, but he shows such restraint when I bathe him or examine his wound. In his eyes are the wits of a man somehow, and I begin to understand Hemwyth's refusal to let him die.

I see for the first time the bond that can grow between a certain kind of man and a certain kind of dog; they both need to lean and be leaned on, and one cannot be called master.

I have never been one attached to dogs; I like all animals equally. With Gunn, it is something else entirely. I find myself carrying in my heart both man and dog. They claim their space at first sight and plant roots. It does not make me happy.

It has been more than two years since the raiders destroyed my village and I came here to Gytha and her world. In that time, I have buried the event and all thoughts associated with it somewhere deep inside where even I cannot find it.

When occasionally sounds or sights resonate within me and threaten to coax memories out of hiding, I thrust them away ruthlessly. My feelings and my father's face I carry around with me like a secret. Always there but never looked at or addressed.

My sister I shut out of my mind completely. I feel her sometimes, like soft wings, beating to be let in.

Those who suffer loss learn soon enough that grief must be curtailed. One must never welcome pain as a permanent guest. The gods have made it so. The passing of days brings relief but not until you have accepted your fate and their right to decree it. This is the wisdom that Gytha tries to share with me, but it sounds ridiculous. I ignore it. I will always ignore it.

I have come to love and respect Gytha and the daily rituals of our lives together as healers and women. I lose myself in their rhythm and view the world through the safe light of order and discipline—until Hemwyth comes along with his voice, his eyes, his dog, and a well-aimed kick that sends it all flying.

After that, I thump through my life like a clumsy bear, bruising all my new edges and getting stung. I go back into the woods at midnight again, crying, raging, and wasting my time, mourning the loss of my family, my people, and my own will.

I am under the complete and unrestrained control of my senses, like a madwoman.

One day I am walking slowly home after gathering wild sage, when a dog comes lunging through the undergrowth.

I am stooped and rubbing his head by the time Hemwyth catches up. From under my hair, I can see him stop a few feet away and just stand there, saying nothing.

The silence grows long, and still, he just stands there while I draw slow breaths and feel everything around me touching my skin. I keep my head down and stroke the soft fur beneath the dog's chin. I think I might be sick.

Hemwyth closes the distance, reaches out for my hand, and pulls me to my feet. He turns my palm upward and traces the flower's mark with his thumb. He looks straight into me.

Such a simple thing to do but it wakes such powerful things; he is stealing something from me, and I am helpless to stop him. All I can do is stare at his lips and know I will go willingly.

In truth, I have little control over what my body chooses to do. I may say nothing, but my eyes do and say what they please. If my skin is silently screaming, somehow, he hears, and this too is out of my control. I am definitely sick with something.

His hands are holding my face, his fingers tracing the dark shadows beneath my eyes and claiming his territory, his work. I breathe in his smell and want to die like that. He places his lips on my mouth and holds them there, still, for a long time while his eyes speak to mine.

Then he is gone, and I am left there, shaken and shaking, thinking I did not understand.

Later, when I arrive home to the hut and Gytha has news for me, I know I must have understood, for it does not take me by surprise.

A betrothal announcement is always a welcome thing in a village. It means that soon there will be a wedding feast, with all its possibilities and pleasures to look forward to.

They will bring out gold, costly furs, beads, and ribbons; greenery will be gathered; and flowers will be cut. There is extra work for all to prepare, but it is cheerfully done. To do otherwise would bring bad luck to the marriage.

On the wedding day, there will be meat, music and dances, and new eyes to measure over tankards of ale. So very much ale.

The gods know I try to drink myself into someplace else, but it is no use. Instead, I sit at the foot of a tree, raising far too many glasses to Hemwyth and his horrible wife, like every other drunkard in the firelit night.

When I have reveled as long as I must, it is more than I can take, and I leave to find my way alone through the dark to our hut. I have long since given control of myself to the night and the gods, so it is a good thing for me that I soon feel the presence of Gunn leading me home.

I collapse into my bed and lie in the dark hut, feeling the room spin and hating everything. I hate him for invading me and hate myself for giving no resistance.

Feeling violated by things that came into my life unasked and left permanent marks—scars. Feeling sorry for myself and crying for my never-ending loss, drowning in self-pity and not even trying to swim.

Then Gytha is stroking my hair as the sun rises and comes through our doorway—a dawn I am familiar with, one that brings me no good. Like every dawn, it is one that I hate.

I fight, as always, and this time, I am allowed to sleep. I sleep for two days and nights, wake to swallow broth and ale, and back to the depths of darkness.

Then some feeling somewhere inside me tells me it is safe to come out. I open my eyes willingly and slowly sit up. From head to toe, I ache, and I need both walk in the woods and bath in the river.

I crouch in the current, let the icy water flow around me, and surrender both body and mind to the coldness. When, a long time later, I climb up to the bank, clouds have covered the sun, and I am as numb as I need to be.

Gytha is waiting with meat and bread—and with words I do not feel like listening to.

"You have carried yourself well, Aela. I did not know you felt it so strongly." She takes my hand gently in hers. "Truly, I am sorry, both because you have endured alone and because I am powerless to help you now, seeing it at last. You will not have come to this willingly, and against such a love, there is no remedy."

I pull my hand free and begin to tear pieces from the loaf. "No? Are you sure? How? Really, how the hell does such a thing happen? Why was I not consulted? Why was I not told that something like this would come so I could at least have prepared for it?"

I slam my hands down. I am so angry. I am so hurt.

Hemwyth goes through my head like a story.

I begin to see how such a thing could happen—with Hemwyth, a giver, a lover of animals. Dogs, horses, and cats all go to him as if they cannot help it, as if he is their family. He always has enough of himself for all of them. How can this be?

People go to him too and tell him their stories and ask for his help like they are lambs, with absolute trust in his ability to fix it all.

How is he never exhausted by them?

When it is remembered that he is, after all, a nobleman born, with a heritage to reclaim and a name to earn, well, what can make him more desirable?

Who could think otherwise while watching him work, fight, and defend? He understands honor because it lives in him. All this is contained in the strongest, cleanest package, with all the right lines—muscle and sinew, warm blue eyes, and honesty. Such simple, unaffected, manly honesty. It is in his voice, resonant and eloquent.

Everywhere you look, you see him—helping someone, holding something up, saving something.

Nothing but a nobleman's daughter is good enough for man like that. It is all that he deserves—and family, since he has none.

I would be happy with a flaw, something I can remember and hold against him when it hurts.

I have no idea how not to love him.

In the meantime, I work on what I can.

I say, "You are wise, Gytha, but you are wrong." I smile at her. "Perhaps it is simply that the remedy is not known to you. It matters little since I will find it or make it myself. I fought these feelings, useless and crippling as they are, and I lost but one of many battles to come. Rest assured it is not my intention to lose often."

These are brave words, and I mean them. The gods might write my fate, but I do not have to submit to it with any kind of grace.

What do I know of these gods who hold such power over me?

They do not like me—that is certain—but I cannot think how I might have angered them. I am young yet; what did I do but listen to my elders and obey commands?

Gytha says the gods do as they please, and it is not for men to wonder at. They may favor one and scorn another; they need not answer for it.

This I can never accept without proof, and she has none. How can anyone know such a thing without reasons to know it? It is beyond me.

She tries as many ways as she can to avoid the question, twisting words and creating her own way out of any kind of answer.

This is knowledge that is had by none, she insists. There are many things about the world we do not understand. We need not know how to create the earth to live contentedly enough in it.

"I am not content enough, Gytha," I say carefully. I do not want to hurt her. "You were a gift to me, yes, but I paid dearly for it, after all. I did not ask to open the door to my own defeat; I do not want to be in thrall to such a man! To any man, in truth, and much less one who is forbidden to me."

Gytha sighs. "I would that you were not, but even you cannot change that you are. Listen to me, Aela: as the days and nights go by, you will heal. So slowly you may not mark it, but still, the hurt will fade as your blood cools and your heart mends. Do not waste the days of your life trying to understand what you will never know."

Because I say no more, she thinks her words have won me.

There are limits to her wisdom.

Chapter 6

I can be stubborn; I admit it. Though some may say otherwise, I am good at concealing my thoughts when I choose to. I let them see what I wish them to see.

So I do with Gytha and the village as I go about my days, doing as I have always done.

I am self-possessed enough not to swerve and change direction whenever I come upon Hemwyth or his wife but not enough to pass him with my eyes open.

I feel his eyes, urgent and hot, on my face, and I feel the coolness that always follows. No one can know that each encounter makes me more desperate than the last.

Each adds its clamor to the intolerable noise in my spirit, and each brings me closer to a day when I might not have the will to control it.

When the slow, endless torture, so softly applied, breaks me and I just let go and scream all the questions and all the words that must never be said.

All the while, my mind is working.

I have more than I want of sifting through the short years of my life, trying to understand them. I sort them out like tangles in thread, patiently and carefully.

I am left with two—no, three—groups of colors: the bright clutch of color that lights the years with my family, the deep darks of violence and loss, and the quiet gray of slow recovery.

For Hemwyth, I have no color.

He is a flame that dances too close and leaves nothing but scorches. I have no way to deal with him. He cannot be placed safely anywhere in my life.

I need to fix it. I am a healer. I look, therefore, to the wisdom of my craft. I know the ways to deal with wounds and illness. I know the effects of plants and other gifts of the world around us.

I have listened, in the darkness around a fire, to the shrunken voices of old women, learning what was never taught to me, things I was not meant to hear.

For all that women say there is no cure for lovesickness and suffer themselves from its effects, I know there must be. They simply have not found it yet.

There are many things to fear in this world. Children's fears are smaller at first, but soon enough, they give way to those that matter. Death has a place at every hearth and endless time to find ways to claim us.

In truth, I am lucky; loss has come later for me than for many. But I have learned well enough to fear love above all. That is where it really hurts.

It is the curse. It is always disguised as a blessing, and we fall for it every time.

The longer you live with it, the harder you hurt in the end. All the sound thinking in the world will not save you, nor will you find solace in your usual places. You are just lost, left there to bleed out.

It is not something I am willing to accept at this time. I will find or make a way.

The time-honored signs by which one can tell any plant from another are unchanging and indifferent tools. They allow themselves to be used for any purpose. I use them to find the secrets of the woods.

I am not a complete fool; I begin slowly and only try new plants that carry the same signs as those I know the use of. Why do I need to tell you this?

After a while, when these efforts have no effect, I begin to combine them, looking for somewhere between drowsiness, dreams, and fire where I can hide.

I know the dangers. I might die or drop and never awaken, like a living death, but I really do not care by this point. I choose to assume that eventually, I will recover, at some point when my blood has cooled.

So I trespass ever more foolishly in the workings of fate, until at last I go too far.

The winds find me in the woods. I am at the foot of a tree, crumbling leaves into the palm of my hand, crushing them into the stain there. I add other fresh leaves, whose moisture binds all.

25

I crush and then slowly lick it all off with long strokes of my tongue, watching the sky darken. Drops of rain shock my hot skin.

I wait with the wind whipping around me, winding my hair and the long grasses together until they sting in sharp lines across my face.

In my mouth, I both taste and feel the bitterness blooming. Death lifts his head, catches a scent, and wakes.

The woods begin to whirl around me. Then Hemwyth's face is a wet refuge in the stormy wild of the night; his arms are like pillars. He is the altar. I am the sacrifice.

"Never, never this," he says into my hair as he carries me.

Blackness comes.

Chapter 7

I open my eyes carefully against the light. Gytha sits there on the floor beside me, stroking Gunn's soft head and watching my face.

I feel the familiar weight in the air on my skin that is the world of pain I know.

Around us lies the evidence of a battle closely fought, wherein both sides feel the relief of victory and the ache of defeat.

"Why does it have to be this way?" I ask.

She looks away. "It is not known. The fates do as they will. This you know, for I have told you more than once." Rising, she begins collecting the bowls and remnants of her struggle.

I clutch the hem of her kirtle. "Stop. Do not walk away, and do not continue to pretend that you know nothing. Sell it to someone who might believe you; I will never." I release her skirt but hold her gaze. "I need to know enough to curse the fates in a language they will understand. If you do not teach me, I will find another way to learn. I swear it."

She stands very still. "Aela, do not ask me to betray the forces that brought you to me."

Her face breaks my heart, but I make myself stay firm and close off mine.

"Aela!" She finds her own firmness. "What I know is precious little, and it would do you no good to learn it. You must trust me to guide you as I see fit. I, whose love you cannot question." These are strong words. Her eyes burn softly, intense black pools of coaxing.

So very hard to resist. I close my eyes and turn my head. "If it were so little, it could not hurt me, Gytha, and if it were enough, you could help me."

I sleep again.

Those who worry for me come to the door, whisper, and leave small tokens—the unspoken words of greens, candles, and small bowls of nuts.

Gytha tells them I have been struck by fever, caught bathing by an unfriendly moon.

People are simple; they believe what they are told. They cannot see that there is no such thing for a woman. All women are born of the moon in the beginning, and she suckles us while we are still in our mothers' wombs, through her skin. Not all women know this.

I do, and I also know that she has her favorites. I can be sure I am not one of them.

Many days have passed, and the ground begins to wake under its winter shroud.

The sun calls the colors from the snow, and I sit on a bench in front of the hut, feeling its gentle heat on my face. Gunn sits beside me with his head in my lap, pressing hard against my hand as I rub his ear.

His tail thumps the ground. I raise my head, and Hemwyth is there, achingly real and blocking out the sun. Every curse and foul word I know goes through my head at the same time.

I say nothing. I freeze the pain as it lights, and when I have mastered it, I rise to my feet.

I stand there, reading in his face the immense relief he gives in to upon seeing me up and aware. He can take his relief and find a place to put it; I will never need it.

Still, I see what it costs him to look in my eyes and say what he says.

"Aela, my wife, Aelfgyfu, is with child. It is not yet her time, yet now she grows wild and fearful. She has not eaten for two days and begins to utter words without sense. Will you come to her? Will you do this for me?"

Gytha clucks and comes to the door. "I will come, Hemwyth. Aela is not yet recovered fully from her fever. Let me gather my things, and I will be there soon."

"No, Gytha, I will go," I say, but when I move into the doorway and go to find my bag, my legs barely hold me up. I shake myself into sense and stop in front of her. "When I return, you will tell me everything you know, Gytha. Everything."

I take my cloak from its peg and step outside.

Hemwyth raises his hand to guide me, but I sweep past him to follow Gunn. There are limits. When we come to his door, I stop and wait for him to enter first alone.

Outside, I come close to turning around. *How can I do this? What will I find in there? How will I do this?*

It is so hard—much harder than I can deal with.

It takes forever for my eyes to adjust to the dim light inside. Aelfgyfu lies on their bed, feverish and moaning, and I put my bag down and stare at her.

I stare and wait for my mind to begin seeing, looking for the signs I must read. But it stops working; nothing comes to me for a long time.

What comes does not help. I feel small wind devils whirling through my head, calling my attention to what it does me no good to feel, stealing my will.

I shake my head and focus. *Raised color? The fever has not yet broken. Eyes are glassy? Her mind is not all with us. Racing heartbeat? No, that is me. Feeling light-headed? She will faint. No, that is me again.*

I bend over her head, letting the blood flow into mine. I press my fingers to her neck, take her pulse, and let the numbers bring order to my thoughts

"What has she eaten in the past few days? Has she had longings for strange things that she will not have eaten before?" Of course she has. "Who has been preparing her food since she is bedridden?"

Hemwyth says, "I have." Just two words, and they are enough to deal with. When he speaks, his voice carries so many meanings that it is hard to focus on the one in his words. It is hard to focus on anything.

He goes on. "I have prepared meat and broth for her, such as any man can make, and nothing that will have been new to her. Before that, I cannot tell you; she cooks as she likes but always well. It matters greatly to her."

"Yes," I say, and I close my eyes, mentally shivering.

I am sure that if I turn suddenly round to face him, I will catch sight of the fates watching me over his shoulder and smiling, dark and elegantly aloof—carefully, cowardly anonymous.

I force my mind back to the woman suffering in the bed. Aelfgyfu has none of the danger signs I know to look for: hollow looks, dark eye circles, and swelling in the legs. She does not bleed, and her fever is not so high as to alarm me.

Gytha has always said that a true healer will know when Death is in the room. He will have come for the battle and to see the look in our eyes when he wins. He is not there, and I am glad since the room is full enough of things that cannot be seen or understood.

I turn to face Hemwyth. "Your wife is not in danger, Hemwyth." It must be the first time I have said his name; I see the shudder as it runs down his body. Who can imagine something like that will move a man?

His eyes flicker briefly toward the woman in the bed and then swing, tortured, back to meet mine. Who knew that blue could burn?

We stand on the hopeless bridge between us, full of things that can never be said or done. Because I know this, as well from my side as his, I step back.

"It is likely something she has eaten or drunk," I say. "It would help to know what and when and if you are sure you gave her nothing new."

"It is as I have told you," he says.

I walk past him to the hearth and corner where the cooking is done. The truth of his words is there in the trunks and cupboards, the hanging herbs and urns.

I search slowly and carefully through every depth and layer, every pot, sack, and box. I find much that other women would not recognize; Aelfgyfu is clearly a creative and resourceful cook, but I find nothing that is new to me, nothing that should not be there.

I walk slowly around the hut, running my eyes over everything I can see.

I see weapons, cleaned and polished, hanging on the wall; leather and rags on a bench with boxes of tallow and tack; and wood stacked neatly against the wall. The place is spare and simple.

Gunn lies by the fire with his eyes closed and his head on his paws, but ears awake and listening.

I come again to the bed. On the far side is a small trunk with an oil lamp and mug of water resting on it. I move them aside, open the trunk, and let its familiar smells rise into me: dried herbs and plants wrapped in fabric, with their sharp fragrances soaking the dark depth of the trunk—medicinals.

I pick up a bowl still musty from the potion it has held, with hyssop, feverfew, and small slivers of bark—the strong scents of lavender, wood lily, and others whose flowers entwine themselves in your head and lull you to sleep. I know this potion.

I have used it myself over and over for a long time now, through long, dark hours, awake and aching, while my spirit wanders, looking for his.

I search for the pot and candle she will have used to call forth the strongest scents. They are not inside the trunk or on the floor beneath the bedframe. I go to the hearth to see if I might find them or some other means of heating the bowl. There is nothing.

Gunn lifts his head, and my hands find his face, absently rubbing his head and neck while I stare into the fire, thinking.

What has Aelfgyfu done with her small collection of medicinal herbs that need knowledge of a kind never found in a cooking room?

I go back to the trunk, sort through them again, and then scrape at the residue left in her bowl. I know it has never been heated. Likely, she drank it. *Poor woman, ill advised by someone claiming knowledge he or she could not possibly have.*

I think about the kinds of effects she should be having, as much as I can know.

Since there is much I do not know, I focus on what I know for certain. All her signs are mild; she is growing calmer, and drops of water form on her forehead.

I rise to my feet and gently try to wake her. She moans and resists. I soak a cloth in the water and wipe her face with slow strokes, forcing her to find me, until she opens her eyes.

Then the healer in me flees. I am Aela, another woman who loves her husband.

She looks out at me from her drugged slumber, straight into my eyes and beyond them to those of her husband. Somehow, she knows. I see the hatred being born in her just before she closes her eyes and shuts me out. This is new to me, this kind of hatred.

I run.

Outside, the sky is black; the trees lit by snow. I stumble blindly through the night, following the dog and followed by the man.

I am close, almost there, when he catches both my arms and stops me. I freeze with a sick weakness in my stomach, all my bones melting, all my wits leaving.

He comes around me, his mouth finding mine. How can I keep him out?

Something somewhere in my head laughs an evil laugh. I don't care. I want to climb inside him and never come out again.

Just dark woods and white snow, shoulders, hands, and powerful, wild feeling.

I know every part of him at once. It is like having forever right in this moment, in this instant.

Gone before I can feel it, see it or begin to understand it myself.

31

Later, when he sits up and gently pulls me with him, he says, "You must go, Aela. I cannot bring myself to walk away from you now, so you must go."

I go with his eyes on my back and blood on my thighs, leaving him behind me. He is mine, and I can never have him. Here is another new hatred.

Chapter 8

I stand before the door to our hut, washed, arranged, and feeling the heat ebb within me.

I call my thoughts to order, thinking of what I will tell Gytha about Aelfgyfu.

I kneel in the snow to give Gunn his rub. I press my forehead to his for a moment, until he grows restless and shifts. Then I go inside.

I give thanks for the dim light of the fire that lights our walls with darkness. That allows me to walk to my bed and sink down into its welcoming, unknowing, nonjudgmental embrace.

"There is no danger for her, Gytha. She will soon recover, and I am exhausted. Please let me sleep, and I will tell the rest in the morning." I raise my head and try to lie a smile at her. Then I close my eyes.

In truth, I am exhausted, but there is no sleeping.

I lie in the dark and feel the profound change in my body as it sweeps through me and unties threads I have been born with. As some things are born, others die.

I come face-to-face with what it really means to not be with Hemwyth.

In one night, I live a world of emotions: wonder, pain, fire, peace, misery, and, finally, dread. After that, I want to stay awake. I know what comes with the sunrise, and I am not going to help it come any sooner than it has to, but eventually, I sleep.

A dream comes to me.

I lie in the woods, in a clearing lit only by moonlight. The gentlest wind causes the grasses and leaves to whisper now and then, but all is quiet around me. I see the soft face of the moon reflected on every branch and stem. I hear the silent swish of the owl's wings before I see him.

He comes to rest on the trunk of a fallen tree near me, flicking his feathers, looking around, and then focusing his gaze on me. I feel the quick flash of fear that prey feels, for an instant, before it gives way to a meaning I can read in his eyes. At once, I understand what I must do, and it makes sense to me.

"I will," I say out loud to him, but he knows already. He takes wing soundlessly, swoops once around the clearing, and then flies off into the dark mystery of the woods. A feather floats slowly down from the sky, and I hold my hands out for it. When I open them, I see it is a white flower, lit in its own pool of moonlight.

I awaken.

The room is cooler now and darker. The coals smoldering in the hearth have lost their warmth and light in the black cold of the deepest night.

I rise quietly and carefully and go to the trunk where I keep the pieces of my own world. I pull the fabric from the bottom, slowly freeing it from the layers on top of it.

On a table, I find the stone and bowl used to grind herbs. I take them, slip my cloak from its hook, and leave the hut.

What moon there was has passed, but her light lingers yet, trapped like the starlight, in the snow and trees. I walk into the silent woods, through black stripes of shadow and waning whiteness.

Finally, I stop, scrape clear the earth with my boot, and kneel on the grasses. I work. I grind the whiteness from the dried bloom, calling the red forth. I add some snow for moisture, and the potion is made.

I carefully wipe the bowl and its stone clean until every trace of dark color is captured in the fragment of fine linen I've used. This I wrap in leather and tie close to my flesh.

I rub the tools through the snow so Gytha will find no trace of their use, dry them on my skirt, and walk back to the hut.

After that, I wait.

Gytha sits in her chair by the door, sorting seeds and planning rows. I crouch on a stool with my bare feet on the warm earth, slowly winding thread onto a spool.

She is looking intently at her work, hoping I will not breach our peace with difficult questions. I am thinking always but trusting myself to know when to ask and what.

When a man approaches along the path toward us, we both let fall our work and stand quickly, tense. More children are due at this time than we are comfortable with.

Only one, thankfully, in the next village. Gytha goes to collect her things, while I clean seeds and thread and marvel at my own stupidity.

How should it matter to me what woman is giving birth? All need our care in equal measure. Still, I can hope that I not be the only one here when Aelfgyfu's time comes.

I have not seen Hemwyth again; I do my best to stay at home, and he does likewise. I know he watches his wife more carefully and takes her care into his own hands.

I need my own recovery. Once I know that I carry no child, I will begin mine.

That night, Gytha stays in the next village. Two more women with pains starting, and the first only just finished and needing urgent care still.

I lie on my bed, restless and alone in the silent darkness, and think about him, having to face her eyes every waking moment. I beg the gods to take pity on him and curse them with the same breath.

On the second evening, I hear the low rumbling of distant thunder that plays herald for our first storm.

Close to twilight, the woods begin to sway, and all the colors darken yet grow sharper the way they will before a storm.

I stand in the doorway, gazing out while the wind slips behind me, tugs my hair free, and sends it flying before my face like a flag.

I begin to walk, mindlessly following the curves of the wind as it winds its way through trembling young trees. Finally, I sink to my knees, and the woods around me go silent. I slowly untie the cord that binds the soft leather pouch and then pull it from the warmth of my waist and wait.

I hear neither warrior nor dog approach. How should I? They are just there.

He fills everything, so I can be aware of nothing else, just his smell and his skin. Mine the moment he kneels. He runs his hands up my arms to my shoulders, crouching beside me and finding my neck with his face.

We stay like that for a long time, motionless, while the bonds between us tangle themselves. Only the storm releases us, sending icy drops of rain to cool the sudden heat and remind us that time is not ours.

I place one hand on his face and guide his gaze to my other; he watches as I unfold the leather square to reveal the scrap of linen inside.

"You must take this, Hemwyth," I say quietly and seriously. "You must wear it next to your skin without removing it until the next full moon. Then, when she shows her white face in the eastern sky, you must steep this small cloth in river water, in your own drinking vessel. Let it be still

35

until she begins to wane in the west, and then remove the cloth and drink the water. All of it."

I keep my face still and hold his gaze, making sure he knows how important this is. His strong fingers rub the fabric; his eyes are willing prisoners.

"And the fabric, Aela? Is it to be kept? Such a scrap as this will be easy to misplace, I think."

I close my eyes, loving his voice and everything I know he is, everything about him. "Dry it, and return it to me, Hemwyth, when you can."

With one hand, he folds it into the depths of his tunic, while the other counts my pulse and leaves memories on my neck.

Then he is kissing me, and I am trying to draw him into me with all my strength. I take as much as I can bear and then break away.

We draw slow breaths, accepting the unspoken reproaches of the gods. This is a serious sin that can never be completely hidden. We are both far too vulnerable, far too human.

We rise together and, with Gunn following, begin to walk back to the village, followed by the fresh, dark power of the storm.

We walk out to our separate ways.

I close the shutters and door and bank the fire. Then I lie on the floor in the center of the darkness and surrender my senses to the wild forces circling the hut.

I am not afraid. I am not one who fears the rages of the gods when they claim the skies and look for victims. I know better.

I lie still, trying to forge armor from my pain.

I close my eyes; the lightning plays on my eyelids. The hammer comes down, and the ground beneath me trembles.

I call out to the gods, "I am coming to find you. And if I cannot make you learn to fight honorably, at least I can make you pay. Something. Somehow."

I am so brave.

Chapter 9

Spring comes, and babies are born. The gods smile on most of the women, but there are a few who just suffer, and it is heartbreaking and exhausting to help so helplessly.

We bury one—just a girl, really, who should not have been pregnant in the first place, being still a child herself.

What a sad, sick thing it is. I can cry out against it forever, and still, it will go on, as it has for centuries and as it always will.

I focus on spring being born around us. By the time the small shoots begin to climb out of the warm earth and into their new world, there are but two babies yet to be born. We keep our bundles ready by the door and carry on with the tasks of late spring.

The days grow longer, and twilight, always a sacred time of day for me, takes on a new, vibrant intensity that makes me love and worship it even more.

It is quiet; things are finding their way home. Even the wind looks for a place to sleep. I sit on the floor in the doorway, listening to the night. Gytha lays violets and crocus blooms out across a board to ready them for drying in the next day's sun.

Then I see Gunn padding silently toward me, it hits me like a punch to the belly. I feel flushing hot and then see that the dog is alone. My pulse slows, but the sick feeling in my stomach stays. I ignore it and let my face flood with warmth. I rise to welcome him.

"Come, Gunn. I am sure I have something for you here from our supper."

He, with the manners of a guest, takes his bone outside and lies beside the door, grinding it into shards. I rub his head and pick leaves and twigs from his fur. My hands find a leather cord around his neck that is unfamiliar to me, but before I have untied it, I know what it is: a square of leather, tied in a bundle.

I unfold it and find a scrap of fabric wrapped around a warrior's plait and stained with drops of his blood. *God in heaven.* I feel weak-headed, gut sick, warm, and cold at the same time. I feel awful—and amazing.

What would any woman feel? I know what it is and what it means.

I press his gold hair to my lips, close my eyes, and hurt very much.

Then I carefully wrap it again, lean forward, lay my head on Gunn's back, and bury my hands in his fur. He raises his head briefly, sniffs at my hair, and then returns to his bone.

When I can, I stand up, cross to my trunk, and open it. I have work to do now.

I have been saving scraps of fabric and bits of twine, keeping them back from the box where such items go to be repurposed. I take them to the corner where we keep our store of medicinal herbs and lay them out on the trestle.

I begin taking a few measures of each and making little piles in the centers of the cloth squares. I tie each up securely into a small pouch or bundle. Those that may easily be confused for others I mark with a small symbol.

At last, when I rise to fetch the new leather pouch I have made for these little packages, Gytha stops her work and comes to stand beside me.

"What is it you do here, Aela?" She waves at our bags near the door. "Such herbs as are needed have long been packed."

I continue slowly and carefully filling the pouch and then winding its cords around it until I am certain it will hold. "I am packing, Gytha, for the journey I will be making when the last baby breathes his first. You will not need me after that." I turn to face her and take her hands in mine gently so she will understand that I am beyond any objections she may make. "You have known I would go one day. My family's blood calls out for justice, and I cannot refuse. Who will avenge them if I do not?"

She shakes her head, frustrated, and looks at me closely, carefully, as one does when talking to small children or madmen. "Aela, you are a woman. Not likely to prevail against any strong man, much less a warrior or a god! What will you do if you find such? You cannot hope to fight them, so how will you punish them?"

"Gytha! Why have I spent these years in training and preparation if not for this journey? Would you have me stay here and suffer quietly to the end of my days?"

She shakes her head. "If I had you trained, it was only as a precaution against such dangers as there always are for women in a world of men. Where you wish to go, you will find far more. Ruthless, determined men, and women too, with means beyond your ken. In the end, you will but trade one kind of suffering for another. Trust me."

"I will come out even then, but I will have tried." My father's shade shivers along my skin. I lift my chin. "There is honor even in the attempt to fight forces you know to be larger than yourself. Forces that can easily defeat you. The gods themselves have told us, you have told me."

I clasp her shoulders with my hands, trying to make her feel the simple truth of my words. "Gytha, if you love me, you will tell me what you know and make my search easier. You know that if it falls within my control, I will return to you here."

She looks at me bitterly; there is no response for such an honest lie.

I reach to hold her, and then I take her hand and lead her to the hearth. Embers light her gentle face with the sorrow of waning light.

"I have asked you many times about these gods whose decisions seem to control our lives with no apparent reason, meaning or thought. You never tell me." I crouch down to look in her face. "You may be content to submit without question, but I am not."

I shake my head slowly. "I cannot. I will not grow old by the fire, never knowing what will hurt me or when or what scars I will carry with me when I leave this world for the next. I will find these gods, and I will ask them what purpose they have in tormenting us. How do we deserve to be treated like this? I need to know why. There can be no sentence without crime, accusation, and witness. I am going soon, Gytha. I ask that you do not attempt to stop me in any manner, and I insist that you tell no one. If you will not help me, I cannot force you, but I demand that you do not judge me."

She looks at me with her ancient eyes, and I see that all this too she has known.

But the gods, whose playthings we are, do not want me to look for them. They do not like to think of being accountable, so they send the first baby to call Gytha to the next village. I am the only one left in this village.

They rip me from sleep that night.

Hammering at the door in the early hours, when fear leaps out from the cracks in the walls.

Me, blinking and stumbling through fog both physical and mental, while Hemwyth guides my steps a new kind of urgency in his hand on my arm.

The hut is hot, the air thick with the smoke and powerless light of many candles and a generous fire. Gunn pants by the foot of the bed. I look beyond him to the white, weak, unlucky woman on the bed.

I am too late. Above her, I see her shade rise as it slips away into the night.

Death does his last bow, smiles, and dances away. I stand there frozen with hate and helplessness.

Then Gytha's voice whispers in my head: *Aela! Remember that in such cases can the baby sometimes be saved if actions are taken quickly and carefully.*

I move swiftly to the side of the bed. Hemwyth comes closer and then stops with no idea what to do. I feel for a pulse I know is gone, then turn swiftly away, and before he can stop me, I pull his blade from its sheath, turn back, and begin carefully cutting a line high on her belly.

He cries out, as I know he will, and stops my hands with his, both clasped hard around mine, reluctant warning in his eyes. I keep his gaze and watch it yield carefully, stepping slowly, to the idea of what might yet be. All this happens in an instant, and then he is placing my hands on her belly to learn what I can.

I feel a flutter of movement, and he knows it instantly. I push as hard as I dare and find a small head where feet should be.

I know then why her blood has long been wasting on the bedding below her. Babies riding like that are always difficult to birth. What I cannot know is how or why the unfriendly eye of some god came to rest upon her. But I can guess.

I begin, looking carefully but quite blindly, cutting a line around the baby within. When I can reach, I squeeze his small body hard, pull him forth, and slide my finger into his mouth to remove what might obstruct his breath.

"Hemwyth! We must wrap him quickly in warm blankets; those by the hearth will be best. Shake them first!" I lay his small, slippery body in the linens on the bed and rub him firmly until I feel his small chest swoop outward for his first breath, lifting like a bird as it takes wing.

Then he is wailing the young warrior in him, feeling his helplessness and hating it.

I tie and cut the cord that ties him to his mother. Then I wrap him tightly in the warmth of soft linen and rock him gently to soothe him.

Hemwyth stands by the bed, looking down at the woman who has given her life for her son. He pulls the covers gently over her mangled body and turns his aching eyes to me. "I have seen countless dead men on the ground after battles; never has it looked like this." His quiet, beautiful voice is mute with pain. "This is a price I would willingly have given on my own terms. How is it that she is the one to pay?"

I pull his pain into me, thinking the same of him. I put all the mercy the gods have denied him into my voice and show him a way out of his despair.

"You have still some favor of the gods, Hemwyth, though it looks like their work here. You have lost your wife, yes, but you have a son, and he has wide choice of wet nurse. For his sake, choose one who is willing and content and not one brought by want. He will thrive; he is healthy."

I cradle the baby close and walk to put more water on the fire.

I look up to Hemwyth's conflicted face and watch him struggle with things he has never felt before—desperate new fealty where no oath was taken and a new kind of pain.

I arm him. "Go now. Go find the wet nurse your son needs; he is hungry."

But I hold him with my eyes first, until I find what I need in the depth of his. Then I lower my gaze and release him.

There in my arms, those same eyes looking up at me and tying threads. I look away, knowing it for the gift it is not.

41

Chapter 10

Gytha returns. Both mother and twin boys are resting, the deep, well-earned sleep of the brave and victorious.

"It is a year of warriors, this," she says proudly, as if she had a hand in it.

"Then you can be sure that battle lines are being drawn somewhere," I say.

She retreats behind a wall of silence, pretending I am not there in the room. I let her for the time being.

She goes the next day to see Hemwyth's son and help the women prepare Aelfgyfu's body for burial. I do not offer to go with her, and she does not ask.

When she returns hours later, her face is set dark but lit with promise. She has been listening with all the skill and intent of one whose craft is to know—enough to understand how the gods have laid their pieces. Having been given both, one sees evil portent or hidden gift as one wishes.

Gytha chooses to find that the gods have relented and shown their favor at last. For her, it is quite simple, and the pieces are merely falling in where they should. "How better for it to pass?" She smiles the gentle, holy smile of the newly converted.

She looks at me closely, letting me read it in her face the unexpected twist in story line, salvation sighted. Who can understand what the gods ordain?

Because I love her, I let her down gently. The merest breath of a smile is gone before I can mean it.

"You know, much-loved woman, that this will not come to pass as you wish it. I cannot stay here with Hemwyth."

She tosses her head and looks to the skies for help. *You see her? This is what I struggle with. Every step must be fought for.* She stamps her foot at me.

42

"Are you mad? Why not? When you can see the gods have willed it so! When the same wind blows at once in all directions, and you have but to follow one to follow all."

She begins to calm down, cutting meat and herbs into neat, precise sizes as she prepares supper. "You, Aela, have felt the hand of a god more than once as it brushed your skin with its cold kindness. I know of no such other person in all that I have heard of the world around us as long as I have lived."

She swings her pot onto the hook over the fire, wipes her hands on her skirt, and smiles at me gently. "It is not in you to deny a gift when it is given. And if you will not think of yourself, what of the son without a mother? To him an indifferent wet nurse while the warrior hunts and the hearth grows cold? You cannot wish it."

She crosses to me and takes my face between her hands. The black tenderness of her eyes seeps through me, putting my wits to sleep and my will to test. "For no other reason but that you love him, Aela. As he does you."

Because I am human, I let this simple truth fracture my heart for a moment, but I know better than to walk where led by a hand I cannot see.

"Yes, Gytha, for that very reason, if no other, I must leave. We have seen how ruthlessly the gods deal, yet because they give with one hand as they take away with the other, we are content."

My face gets hot; I am so frustrated. I take a deep breath and count to thirteen. "We are bought and sold in a bargain where we play every role but winner. Why should we accept this? Over and over again, simply because it amuses them?"

She steps back. "Aela, child of my heart, you are wiser than your years allow, I give you, but you are very wrong to struggle thus. Would you expect their favor for free then? Should they not be paid when their efforts bear fruit? There is nothing to be had in this world or the next without price. This you know."

She considers the argument won, so I am forced to means I would never otherwise employ.

"Pain is free, Gytha. And sorrow. Of these you may have as much as you like; there is unlimited supply, whether you will it or not. And why should they choose such a method of payment? Surely they can find other ways."

She has no answer for this, so supper is eaten in silence.

43

After, she rests while I clean our things carefully, thinking hard, knowing that my words can both reassure and terrify. Finally, we sit before the dying fire. Before I can speak, she calls it forth herself.

"I will tell you what little I know, Aela. But first, you must promise me one thing in exchange. See Hemwyth yourself, and tell him where you go and why."

It feels as if the earth falls away from me, and there I am, backed into a corner with no escape, starting to fall. As much as I say I am not stupid, I believed I could just go like the sun at twilight, when it sinks suddenly at the end.

It takes you by surprise when the darkness claims you—every time.

One day he would wake up, and I would be gone.

I cannot believe she would use me against myself like this.

She goes to find him. I look to the skies for somewhere to hide.

He leaves Gunn outside, closing the door gently on his anxious face. Gunn whimpers. So do I.

I watch him come to me and learn new ways to suffer.

He sits on the stool next to me with his elbows on his knees, leaning toward me. The glow of the embers lies on his skin like a lover. I am jealous of it.

My eyes drink. His eyes are dark and clear; they find their way inside me and show me how simple it could be.

How I love his face.

I find a long scar on his wrist and trace it desperately with my fingertips, willing my senses to be still. Because I know how powerless I really am, I focus my gaze on it and put words between us. I start, slow and subtle.

"There is much we do not know, Hemwyth, of each other and much we need to. Will you tell me? Talk to me of yourself, and then I will do the same." I smile at him, trying to make it look easy. "Perhaps we might come to understand how and why we are bound together like this, so perfectly and painfully."

He smiles back and tries to lift my chin so he can see my face better, but I resist. His hand comes to rest on my arm in an exquisitely warm reproach. Then he leans back, and I can breathe again.

He turns away from the hearth, so his face is lost to the shadows. I am grateful; it will be hard enough not to go up in flames when I hear his voice. I close my eyes and let it weave its way through me.

"I have lived in this village for over eleven years, Aela. In that time, I have had but one calling. One purpose. And everything I do leads me toward it." He looks at me sideways. "I am a warrior. Nothing more and nothing less. I fight for Hengest and learn how to defeat an enemy. I learn how to keep my family and my home safe." His eyes do not flinch. I do. He turns away again. He talks, and his words come and find my heart.

He tells me about his mother, who came into his corner one afternoon, smiling and beautiful like she was, and had him pack his things for a journey to a neighboring village. She watched him with hidden eyes, trying to untie things. He felt it like a presence, without understanding it, until he did.

She let him bring all his weapons, his slings, and his dice. What his father did not know would not hurt him. She even let him bring his dog.

He thought they would go together, but she stayed, and they were lighting the torches as he rode away. The flames made a taper of her by the gate, with her long white dress, white face, and gold hair. The taper made a picture that he carries with him always.

He rode into the dark woods and out of a world he would never see again.

"It is simple," he says. "My uncle, Siric, sits in my father's chair; his family sleeps in our chambers. It is a wrong I must right; as long it continues, I cannot raise my face. How can I? Why should I?" He twists his palms together. I am mesmerized by the play of light and shadow on his arms. The strength in them makes me weak.

He turns his eyes to me. "I am yours now, Aela, but you know I have a son, and a duty that comes before everything, even him. Even you. And I would never be worthy of you if I left my father unavenged and my name worthless."

He might have saved himself the breath; I am not listening. I am caught, locked in love and lust, pain and hunger. My heart aches for him, but the rest of me just wants him.

His smile forgives me, but he pays me back, resting his warm golden hand on my thigh. I light instantly; he sucks in his breath, and we both recoil.

He reaches out suddenly and frees my hair. His strong fingers lose themselves in tangles; he holds my face with both hands like a sacrifice.

I stay still, trying to breathe, and he begins to undress me slowly. I love him enough to let him. My skin surrenders unconditionally, awake, alive, and willing.

I undo his belt, and he helps me pull his tunic over his head and off.

45

All the lines of muscle and sinew that make a warrior, the sleeping strength, the scars that run in mysteries through flesh and hold stories, they speak to me in a language I have never heard before but instantly understand. I feel his warmth under my hands; I taste his skin. I breathe in his scent, and my heart leaps to find his.

I want to be conquered by him—now.

I just want to give him everything.

The night and the world fall away, and we are the storm.

After the storm comes the perpetual dawn like the enemy it is.

We lie, limbs entwined, skin-damp and trembling, on the bare earth of the floor, remembering who we are.

I tell him I have my own work to do; I do not need to explain.

We are trapped in this place and this time. The gift must be placed carefully and reluctantly back in its box and kept for another time.

When a small son looks for eyes he remembers, he will find some other.

Each battle survived, for a loyal warrior, becomes a countdown toward a day of justice.

For me, I know that such a day happens only if the gods will it. Often, even then it takes little to send the wind after it. As long as this remains true, each day that I live, I will search.

Chapter 11

I awake suddenly from a heavy sleep. The door is open to the full, glorious beauty of the moon as she rises over the eastern woods.

I see that Gytha has put aside our stools and swept the floor. It is newly clean and smooth, an altar for the moonlight.

She has drawn a large, perfect circle, with its telltale mark in the center. She holds both wands and string as she kneels in the circle. She places them crosswise on her knees.

The moonlight winds its tendrils through me, and I am kneeling too now.

"Use your mind, Aela," she says, "to see from the sky. Let it carry you higher and higher into the darkest reaches of the night sky, and look down." She whispers, keeping her words from hidden listeners.

Because she is Gytha, she will have left nothing to chance. I feel the pungent tang and tug of familiar herbs as they smoke silently in their pot. They seep into my mind, right through my open windows, straight to my spirit.

I begin to know things I have not been taught. I see the unseen and hear what I cannot hear—the language of life and the sound of time. I feel the pulse of the earth, and my own heartbeat runs with it. This is our craft. The moon is our goddess.

Gytha picks up the wands and hangs them around her neck by their string, claiming her place in the line that stretches both far into the past and as far into the future as the world itself will last. The line by which she is connected to me, so that she is more mother to me than my own.

We are a line of true healers, and in truth, neither are we born, nor can we die, for we have always existed, as we do still and always will. A thread that runs through time, part of a tapestry that includes many such unknown, unperceived threads. She bares her shoulder. I raise my palm.

There in the room, beside us, comes the silent shade of another. He is my captive yet not. Is it a sacrifice if a victim is willing? He is the true color of his own blood. I will answer for it; I will heal for him.

Gytha hisses and shakes her head at me. It is too late to undo what I have done.

I am not worried. "He will not know. This I tell you."

She is not pleased. She does not like to be surprised. She begins to draw in the sand with one of her wands. She mutters.

"I must own that you have gift of some knowledge not taught you by me; it is strange that you should know this." She pauses. "Yet secrets tell their own nature by name. And that too is a test."

She looks into me with the eyes of a cat, black and feral. She needs to know. I could not move if I tried. I cry out, "Gytha! Many have shown me—you among them. Am I blind, deaf, and dumb? You know well then which cautions I will have used. His mind, very much a man's mind, will not willingly look for that which he cannot see or fight. He will tire when he thinks of such things, and sleep will overcome him, as it does all men, at all times. I have made certain of this. I only wish to bind him and to keep him safe."

She smiles ice. "Do not mistake yourself as to such a man. He is as different from his kind in his own way as you are from yours."

She forces my gaze down to see the story she has drawn in thin, sharp lines on the ground. Here and there, sand is mounded gently in curves and corners. My mind engages instantly, as it always does, in the dance of light and shadow.

I read the patterns for myself immediately; she does not know this, nor do I wish her to. I listen and pretend otherwise.

My mind leaps ahead as she leads me down ravines and up mountains. I find every carefully concealed crevice, subtle web, and hidden ambush. I listen intently, prepared for them. My face has been trained to betray nothing.

I disregard them. I light the flames of invisible ink. I look, listen, and learn.

At the end, I am told that I must forget all I know yet never forget that I know it. I must share it with none, though it might be inscribed on my soul for all to see who can. I am told that I must never act against it, even as I am shown the path to follow and the lie it serves.

It will do them little good to hide the door.

I will see what I must not see, and I will use every power in me to find where I cannot be allowed to go. I will ask the questions that should and must be asked, or I will perish in the attempt, and in that I will have an answer.

I want to go—before the cries of a newborn, too familiar and blameless, can wreck me.

In truth, I am far more helpless here at home than out in a world unknown to most and in far more danger from something worse than simple death.

Gytha is who she is. If she cannot keep me here, she has at least seen to it that I am well prepared.

Thus, my lessons are diverse. I learn to throw knives accurately enough to please her and how to use them to defend myself. I memorize potions to simulate death and those to command sleep. I practice feigning meek resignation and realistic clumsiness. I chant vague, misleading responses to all manner of questions—the mantras of deception.

I believe I master the way of walking like a man. It is easy to dress as such when one can sew. I learn to imitate men's movements, keep my voice hoarse and my hands hidden. I work until I am strong and until I can be either man or woman in a moment. I am young; I train for the life of an acrobat, a nomadic healer, and a servant. I am given the names of important people to claim if needed, whatever is needed. I am taught how to look boldly into the eyes of anyone, lord or otherwise, as an equal, leave no doubt in one's mind and do it quickly—instantly.

It seems I find it difficult. I am sure that I breathe it so and live it so—that it is so. Gytha cannot see this in my face, she says stubbornly and blindly, even though it is quite obvious. I am the daughter of a chieftain!

"Your eyes say otherwise."

I practice.

I am taught useful skills, such as any young man might know: how to guide and stable horses, how to carry and serve invisibly and efficiently, how to clean and prepare food I might encounter if among the wealthy, and how to eat it.

We make ready a score of stories that might explain my presence alone in whatever situation I might find myself. Small packages are tucked in the corners of my bag—things to embellish my stories, she says. "Look at them, and make sure you know them well."

She talks for hours at length. How should I remember so many things?

"Do not forget the signs of healers, so you may know them when you see them. They will help in all ways they can.

"Remember that you will fare best the less you are seen and noticed. When you cannot help but be seen, be unremarkable. Easy to forget.

"Please, Aela, for my sake, guard your thoughts closely. Think. Will you need to fight every small battle you encounter and thus put off the only one that could ever matter? Let those questions without answer remain so."

She smiles bleakly. "Do not let your thoughts ring forth unbidden and unprepared into the permanence of words."

I take her shoulders in my hands as gently as I can. "Gytha, I am not without wits. Nor am I easily goaded into rash actions. You know how desperately I need to find what I am looking for. You have seen the forfeit. That should be enough for you."

I say this truthfully and bravely, shaking my head hard to keep his image out of my mind.

Gytha ties a dull brown shawl around my head, closing herself off, and steps back. "You must smear some mud on your face, Aela, and keep your hood up. God help you. Taken for boy or girl, you will yet be taken." She shudders and groans, pressing her hand into her face. There is a long, unbroken silence.

She looks at me, tear blind and reluctant but coming finally to understand me.

Chapter 12

I will walk north. Everything that Gytha has judged I will need is in a bundle on my back—perhaps not so much as she liked but as much as I can carry comfortably. I have a knife at my belt, another strapped to my leg, and a few in my bag.

My coins have been hidden in seams, the plait of Hemwyth's hair in its wrap, tied securely around my waist. It is my talisman. Around the top of my walking stick, Gytha has tied a small pouch. She has sewn colored threads and beads in a pattern on the front. This is her talisman.

From inside it, she removes two small wraps of fabric.

"These must be concealed on your body, close to the skin and secure. They will help you, Aela, if you are in dangerous places. One you will recognize as the potion to induce the deep sleep of a trance, which must be put into food or drink. The other is powerful and unpredictable; use it only if you have no choice."

She shows it to me; crumbly brown, and damply fragrant in its fold of fabric. Her eyes are dark and serious, holding me quietly and carefully.

"Only a pinch of this—tossed onto a hot fire, in small places—will summon forth spirits and shades and creatures that do not exist. Light and darkness will dance wildly together; the rules of nature will be broken. Such will be the tricks played upon you in your mind only! You will think the gods are among you; you will be powerless and will not care."

I smile. "Is it then to be used on myself, Gytha, or others?"

She does not smile back. "As you need it, Aela. You will know."

Despite her protests, I am dressed in my tunic and skirt. I begin as myself, a healer.

It cannot be said that I do not give the gods a chance to play fair.

I have horrified her too by not making any attempts to read signs. Choosing my direction at will, she insists, is sure to insult the gods. I cannot help but be amused by this, and now I have added sacrilege to insult.

I walk. I know without looking that Gytha stands in the doorway. She will remain there long after I am out of sight. When she finally, reluctantly goes inside and closes the door, I will know that too, and it will hurt.

The farther away I get from the village, the harder it is to breathe. For a long time, I stumble along, crying like a child, suffering as only a woman can. It takes all my will to keep walking. I am a string wound too tightly; it will take nothing for me to break and turn back.

After a while, my body betrays me, falling to pieces and turning weak, making me work hard for every step, making me pay. I hate everything. In brief flashes, I can hate Hemwyth too for bringing his dog and himself into my life.

I trip on a branch and fall ingloriously and painfully. This is good for me, this joke at my expense.

I brush off my skirts, retie the bundle across my back, and rise with new strength. To distract myself, I count every tree I pass on my left that I can touch as I go by. By twilight, I have had to start anew many times, marking every hundred in a notch on a stick. I keep walking, heading north.

Soon it will be dark, so I stop when I come to a sharply rising hill. I will sleep with my back to its base, as I have been taught. I place my bag on the ground and gather as much wood as I can for a fire. I will never collect enough to last through the night, but the days are long now; the hours of darkness are shorter. It will do. I am so tired.

I find a place where trees grow closely together, near enough to the hill to give me a second wall of sorts. I clear the ground; scrape a small, shallow hole; and then light the kindling. Flames dance into the darkness of the woods around, playing hide-and-seek.

When I have eaten, I offer my stick to the fire and sit in quiet worship until the last light dies and the blackness wins.

I will not say that I am afraid. I remind myself that the sounds of the night forest are friends I have long known. Sleep comes.

In the cool gray of dawn, I feel the warmth of a dog beside me and the flush of the first dawn I have not hated. It feels like a gift, but I know better.

This breaks my heart like nothing else—and almost my resolve. Gunn lies still, silent, and strong while I wrap my arms around him and weep uncontrollably.

Then I see the hand of the gods. I see this first friendly dawn for what it is: the smiling face of a different kind of treachery.

I am angry at first, but then I look into the warm eyes of a friend. I wipe my face on my skirt hem, pull my shawl up over my head, and sleep again until the dawn is no longer a threat.

He is my warrior. Together we walk through the long, hot days of summer, going always north.

He is a hunter; he keeps himself fed, as do I. When we come to a farm or hamlet, I let it be known that I am a healer, and I trade both labor and remedies for as much food as I can carry. Where fortune smiles and none need my help, I ask for news, and I watch for information in all kinds of places.

I sit in great halls and listen to tales told and valor sung, of battles whose outcomes draw deep lines on the earth and divide sons. I hear of new ways for men to destroy one another. I learn all the different names for betrayal. I look for common threads. I remember what I have heard.

We cross over the lands of chieftains, woods, and fields, and rivers so wide and mighty no bridge could span them—rivers that must be crossed.

A ferryman, white-haired and bent, has seen much and knows even more.

I watch him long enough to understand his work, and then I approach him. "Good father, sit now, and rest your bones. Let me hold these for you." I take the ropes from him with just enough strength to convince him and no more. I smile my respect and then lower my eyes; the line between deference and submission can be easy to mistake.

"You have lived through many years, father—what was your trade before you came to be guardian of this crossing?"

He rolls a sleeve and holds his arm out to me; I see the scars of a blacksmith.

We are silent for a moment, watching the water swirl possessively, jealously, around the corners of the ferry. "I am a healer," I say.

It is his turn to smile. "This I know already, daughter, but if I did not, I would guess it by your attention to an old man such as I. It is as it should be." Both he and I know his life to be the treasure it is. He knows too that I will mine it.

Later, we share his ale and my bread and meat beside a small fire in his hut. It is a place of shy shadows and smoke—a place of truth. He tells his version of it.

"There are but three ways to cross the river from north to south or back. All are guarded by ferrymen, as is every river crossing, in one way or another. When called to be a ferryman—do not ask me who calls; I know only who answers—one becomes part of a kinship not forged in blood. One formed by knowledge, bonded to the rivers we serve, those of water and of time."

The length in his eyes takes my breath away; in them is a place one could get lost easily. I am too young for such a door to be opened to me. I am not ready. I twist away.

He smiles gently. "Nothing so mysterious, really. People talk." I hear a hint of resolve in his voice. "Like other goods, knowledge can be given freely or sold. Or traded."

I smile back into his face, so he can see how amused I am. "Or stolen." His smile grows to meet his eyes.

I say, "Then please, father, tell me only what I ask, and I ask for as little as possible to bring me where I need to go."

I let my headscarf fall down around my shoulders and free my hair. I look into his eyes as an equal, quickly, and as a woman, slowly. I fold my hands demurely on my knees and speak softly. I tilt my head so I am looking up when I raise my eyes to his face.

He is ancient, this ferryman, yet I see the effects of my efforts as they pass through his eyes. *Not all mysteries here then.* I sit a little straighter.

"I will ask you three questions, father, and that is all I wish to know at this time, if it so pleases you. Who makes the decisions that inform the fates of men? Where will I find him? And how do you and your ferrymen escape his attentions?"

His eyes are laughing. "It seems your strengths are not those of modesty, daughter, as your false hands declare. It is as well. There are as many kinds of strong as are needed, yours as much as any. So I was when young blood ran in my veins."

I get a glimpse of what that might have looked like; a flush appears across his face, gone before I can name it or yearn for it as one curious mind to another.

He goes on. "You assert boldly that he is he, while there is no possible way for you to know it. You assume as well that we have been free of his interest. This is not so, I assure you. We survive because we endure. We look and listen; we learn. The more we suffer, the more we know." He spreads his hands out. "And so there will be ferrymen far into the future, even when they cease to call us so. We endure, and we are strong."

He does not frighten me, nor do his words, eloquent truth or otherwise. I do not frighten easily.

"Yet you must grant that he is he, good father. And you will tell me of him. All that you know of my enemy, you will tell me. And then you will show me where to find him." For this, I must go further than is wise. I hold his eyes, forcing them to recognize his contender as such. "It is in your own best interest to help me find him; this you know. At worst, it will affect you little; in truth, your life can only improve. Even if I fail, at least you will have learned."

He ignores this even as he yields to it, sighing. "There is a god—Lord Pandor, as he must be called—who rules the forces of chaos. In truth, it is not so much he rules them as he made them. They serve him, and they are him. He is them."

I cut him off. "What? What does that mean? As you are a ferryman? And I a healer? It sounds like nothing of sense to me."

He laughs the dry, humorless laugh of the old. "Let it go, please. It and he—damn me, it must be he and it—are nothing like us or this." He shudders, but reluctant admiration is difficult to conceal in a place of truth.

I have never been one to grant unlimited or unknown control of myself to anything. A silent voice whispers in my ear, calling me the liar I am. I stand firm. The truth of this place has no claim on me, it is not my truth. I will know it for the sacred when I see it.

Tonight there is time enough to learn more, of this god, my enemy, so I will listen to the ferryman, but I do not have to trust him

He places my hands together, palms up, with the left resting in the palm of the right. He raises my thumbs and joins them at the tip. He folds his own around mine, locking them in for a moment.

"Hold your hands thus while I speak of things concerning your unfortunate, obstinate obsession. I will do likewise. I will tell you what I know of Pandor. If you are then so witless as to wish to continue on your fruitless, fatal journey, I will not stop you. If you seek to remember something I have said, place your hands in this position, and they will guide your memory." He sits back on his stool.

I shiver slightly, and he leans to put more wood on the fire. While he is turned, I pull a small scrap of fabric from beneath my sleeve; it lies in the palm of my hand like a blessing. I hide it from him.

He begins to talk plainly and simply. So easy to believe we are alike, he and I, in our passion to make something, or someone, answerable. If there is a tremor in his hand or a waver in his voice, I know them for the weapons they are. We are, none of us, beyond any means for our cause of choice.

He leads me a long way down a busy road, but in truth, I do not move much in the end. He gives me vague references that remain unfinished, descriptions of something or someone I will never have seen before.

"Has he then wings?" I ask impatiently. "Is there a beast within him?"

He sighs, "No, but yet he is very different." *Well, any fool would know so.*

"He has never been seen by human eyes. Do not ask me how this is known." He is doing his best to confuse me now, words without substance, without number.

By now, my spine is getting rigid. He deals so lightly with sacral truth that I might think he takes me for a simple woman. I press my hands together tightly, feeling the sting and flush of hot blood. I look in my head for Gytha; her face calms me. I call her words forth, and they are *patience* and *power*—forever entwined and seldom employed together. I smile and ask him, "How can we know that such a man exists? What are the signs that betray his presence? How does he manifest? How is he perceived? How does one become aware of his presence? Does he ride with storms wildly or come quietly and invisibly like the fog, creeping in silence along the ground until you are pinned beneath him and helpless?"

I stop, vexed to be betrayed by my own lips, singing my weakness and wasting words—again.

I will practice.

The ferryman talks long into the night, and I begin to know a little of the one who took my family. As befits a god, he lives in a mountain fastness far to the north, where he does not trouble himself to calm the winds. Steep ridges and sharp crags, marshlands of green miasma, holes with no bottoms—thus did Pandor carelessly throw together his lands long ago, when the earth was born, and thus they remain, uncrossed by mere men.

He drinks and then passes the horn to me carelessly and dismissively.

In his face, I read the mistake he makes. He has chosen to see me as being far more mere than ever a man could be. There can be no hope for a woman where men have failed. So he relaxes.

The fire is high now. I look at his eyes, watching them watch my hand, as I slowly lean toward the flames. Fist closed, flick wrist, open hand, and set the truth free. He cries out, and the wind breaks in.

Flames turn black and shadows blind. Lights flash as they die. Out of the dark fire, I see a white face with black eyes-- both tortured and cruel.

Around him black flames rise, and in them are the ruins of ancient cities, rivers of blood, and forests of hidden death.

I hear a sound like thunder screaming, and suddenly he is there, alive in his own eyes, that meet with mine and widen in shock. I see him, and he *sees* me, only for an instant; but it strikes me like a blow. I cower in instant submission, a shameful gut reaction. I hate myself.

I look up, and the vision is gone. My eyes close, and as my racing heart slows, I feel the scar form within me. I hate it, but I must carry it whether I will or not. This I understand to be the price.

The ferryman sits like a statue. He has had his own vision; he wears it still in white skin and glazed eye. When he finally looks at me, I am someone different now to him. He turns from me with unfeigned tremor and new things to learn.

He claims he has nothing more to tell me, and nothing I say changes his mind. Tearful entreaty, brutal sense, unspoken threat—all alike are useless. He sleeps while I smolder in the dark, lost in the chaos of my own thoughts.

Dawn brings her merciless light, and my eyes yield yet again without a fight. I am weakest always when and while the sun rises. I curse her.

The ferryman sits by the hearth, waiting. He shows me a bucket of steaming water, soap, and a piece of linen. He leaves the hut to me and a need at once newborn and ageless, unperceived and painful—that I might be both clean and warm together at once. A rare and precious thing for a woman who bathes in rivers.

I wash with the slow strokes of order—rhythm, repetition, and numbers. Thoughts fall into place; I see clearly what I know, what I must yet learn, and how far I have yet to walk.

When I have combed the wet tangles from my hair, I confine it once again to braids and hood. Outside, the ferryman sits on the bank by his pier, a basket of food and jug of ale at his feet. We eat in silence for a time. I am pleased to see him offer Gunn his share.

I thank him for sharing his hearth with me, the debt has been noted, and I press a small pouch into his hand. It is little enough; the relief it will offer to aging bones is, like all relief, fleeting.

He gives me a small bundle of fabric rolled tightly in a cylinder and tied with a leather thong. He makes me hold it with both hands and places his over mine. "These, I know, must always and only be given. Take them from me, Aela, and may they help keep you on your path. To the north always, as you have done."

He lets me see in his eyes his absolute belief in me and in my quest. It lingers in my mind like shards of light in falling water. I am still blinded by it long after I have lost sight of the river behind me. I walk firmly onward. I think, *how did he come to have my name then?*

Chapter 13

I keep northward, but unlike before, when I took the straightest ways and easiest means to go north, now I walk from village to village. Sometimes going far out of my way, so that more than once, I find myself lost. I look to be among people, as many as possible, always.

Now I am a young man who holds his own in the crowded markets of villages, throngs of the great halls, tents of armies, and anxious fields of harvest. A young man and his dog.

Somewhat shy, fond of the edges and dark corners but a willing hand with quick work and a good listener.

I, Affa, am learning that listening is the most valuable skill of all.

For all that men whisper in the presence of alchemists, they are but different names for the same thing. So it is with priests, astrologers, healers, ferrymen, wise men, masters, and slaves—listeners all.

I learn too that in a man's world, you are only as powerless as you allow yourself to be.

This does not surprise me.

If at night my woman's heart hammers out the lie, I endure it quietly. If alone in the darkness I drown myself in Hemwyth, this is nothing to the light of day. It will not show on my face.

When I have time to spare at twilight, I kneel at the foot of a tree with Gunn on watch beside me and close my eyes on the world around.

I listen to the dogs of dusk. When they are silent, I hear the lone singer, the twilight bird, who sings his soul into mine.

When the wind comes and puts them to sleep, I know that night will fall swiftly now.

I call up his face. In the white skin and the black cold of his eyes, I look for the lord in him. I try to imagine what kind of being he is. Though he might be shaped as a man, he could be anything in truth.

How does one battle such an enemy? What weapons could be used?

I do not imagine a test of arms; this war will be fought with wits. My wits tell me already that I am outmatched before I have begun and that arms may well be used. Gytha sends her whispers echoing through the halls of my mind. I cannot hope to prevail. Home waits.

My head, my heart, and my treacherous, burning body all sing with increasing intensity. I am held, weakening, in their song, happy to surrender.

Finally, when I can feel myself breaking, I open the doors to my father and my family; my sister, Ymma; and the lost, swirling faces of the unquiet dead. The stark wind of pain sweeps through me, and everything in its wake is frozen hard.

It is time to sort, I think. I gather the threads in my mind and begin to lay them out. The picture will form slowly, as always.

What I know, what I can begin to understand, and what I can guess. I find patterns and remember faces. I cast my thoughts outward like gossamer threads in a web of truth.

I call to mind pictures, seared into memory, of every ravaged village and field of carrion. I see them scattered across the land, draw lines between them, and catch the faint, lingering scent of blood.

For every epic hero, there is an evil villain. There are victims. There will be also lust and gold, jealousy and cowardice, and something called honor.

A word with one meaning that means many different things to those who use it. For all that it is ruthlessly defined and brutally enforced, it is rarely seen.

I wait to see evidence of it existing at all. I will earn it, if I can.

In the meantime, my wits have led me here to this village on the riverbank, with its houses of stone and strange temple. Straight-lined streets full of crooked life.

One day I hover at the edge of a square, watching a busy innkeeper take on more than he can deal with at once. I look for where I can be useful; I see casks of ale and wine in plenty to be unloaded but none that I could lift. I hate this truth, as I hate most of them.

I wait for the unmanly flush on my cheeks to wane before I step forward, take hold of two poultry crates, and begin to bring them around to the back for the innkeeper, who pays the driver carefully but keeps an approving eye on me.

His smile becomes genuine when I engage a place for the evening. I read his face—*a paying customer now. Come. Any excuse for a drink, eh? My new friend? Have your first one on the house. Why not? You're a good fellow it is plain to see.* His gaze takes us both in, but he has no greeting for Gunn. I know it for the mistake it is, and it puts both of us on guard instantly. I pay for three nights in advance and let it be known that my dog sleeps with me.

I begin my usual practice in these sorts of places: ears open, mouth shut, quietly useful and a tiny bit clumsy. I must make him glad enough to have me around but not so much as to want to keep me.

This is my first attempt as a man in such close quarters for an extended length of time. I focus hard to remain always in character. My cheek is shadowed at sunset; I spit in the dirt and wipe my face on my sleeve.

I watch myself too closely, so I do not see trouble coming.

In the dark of night, needs sometimes arise that must be dealt with quickly and without Gunn. I make him stay and take my walk alone.

I am sleepy and unprepared to be slammed against a wall and rudely assaulted by a hand that leaves no doubt it knows I am a woman.

He leans his weight on me; I am crushed to the wall with my hands pinned between. His head presses mine hard to hold me still, and he struggles with the ties of my leggings. It takes long enough for me to understand why men prefer women in skirts, and it gives me time to gather my wits.

He curses me, fumbling, and I know his voice—a man with just enough evil in him to follow where led, as others have done, as he is told. Evil was never born in him, nor can he create it, but he can perform it. I know how to deal with him. One without imagination is the best of foes, the easiest.

I give him what he wants; I know it better than he does.

He has exerted himself, after all; he has fought for it.

I stop struggling and freeze. I stay that way, letting him feel that I am clearly struggling with myself now; it is all I can do to remain motionless.

He pauses, taken by surprise, and then pushes harder against me. I feel his strength building as he loses patience with simple fabric. He will rip it from me soon.

Just before he breaks, I let myself go limp in his arms, boneless and resigned. I give the slightest shiver. Now he is really confused; he reacts with greater force, and I tip the scales and go willingly, from fearful to frozen, from soft and yielding to almost begging. He must be seen to be winning.

Later, he will ask me why I pretended to be a man, though he saw through my disguise soon enough. More observant than most, he does not like the idea that appearances can be so deceiving. How is a man to know then?

I tell him that every woman prefers to have some control over whom she beds and why.

The man he is makes the connections; he stands a little taller.

I wash carefully, return to my corner, and pull Gunn close to me. I draw the blanket over my head and let the insult slowly fade from my body. I did not ask to be taken in such a personal, intimate way, but in truth, it is just a different move in the same endless game.

It is little enough to pay for such a key.

Chapter 14

I have been looking for him or someone like him. In time, I would have seen the signs as they showed themselves. I would have known them, though I have no idea what they might be. How do you search for what you have never seen?

Something would have called me; the collected wisdom of ageless healers is never silent.

I found it in his eyes.

There are only two ways to see into the soul of a man.

The first is through his eyes, when his body arches above you, sure of conquest but still needing to own it. You must allow yourself to submit in some way, or you will never see. His windows open briefly—it is so hard to catch—when he wins. He cannot help it. He must announce it. He does not know it.

The other way is also through his eyes, as his shade leaves him. What do his eyes say while he is dying? A truth of such consequence that no one pays it the slightest attention.

I did not look for it in Hemwyth. I had no need to; I could read it on his skin. It left traces for me.

But I was watching the blank shallows of a faithless innkeeper's eyes as he stroked and preened himself on my body, and when he could not help it, the shutters flew wide, and I saw the black flames of the black god he serves.

I awake with new purpose.

Now all his actions must be seen differently—every friendly word, every bargain struck, every careless mistake—and he must be courted, captured, and held without his knowing.

He wants Affa to leave and Aela to come in his place. He will protect me, he says.

I am happy to comply. When I return, none will connect the boy with the woman. I will make it so. I will paint the features of every wanton woman on my face, and then I will try to hide it.

I will think of Hemwyth, and my eyes will glow. My hair will shine, my need will show through shape and scent, and men will want me.

Even a man such as him, in thrall to the winds of hell. For all that he serves the gods, he is but a man in the end, like all others.

But he will be the one to have me, in the only way that matters to men like him, and he will strut, beat his chest, and grow fat on the envy around him. When he is torpid and sleepy and the taste of victory becomes familiar and comfortable, he will make a mistake.

I watch him closely as carefully as I can every moment that he is within sight.

His wife hates me with the winter patience of women who have no fight left in them. I have all the weapons anyway, and in such a test as this, her very goodness tells against her.

To be forbidden is to be an unsolvable problem. A man can win only by losing, and he loses when he wins.

It can drive him mad. He is susceptible in ways he does not know. It is every woman's duty to exploit this.

There is nothing I could say to his wife that she would accept, least of all the truth.

I work silently and watchfully. And when her words are harsh, they have no sting in them for me. I mourn for her, knowing how alone she is. Nothing can ever change that for her. She is another quiet casualty, insultingly anonymous.

If nothing else, his work is consistent and efficient.

I pour the heat of my waking anger into my arms, kneading the weak flesh of the innkeeper's back, arms, and legs. He loves this, but when I am too thorough, he gets restless. He finds my eyes, and I lead him elsewhere.

There is much to be learned in different ways from one body to another, skin to skin.

When you lie with a man, you are under his hands. How you are handled, what marks he leaves on you, these cannot be feigned. They tell.

But he is canny, my innkeeper; he keeps his secrets close. He is a man who does not lightly jeopardize his livelihood. I must do more than I am, but I cannot think what.

I wait for the moon. I unwrap my wands and make the circle. When I feel her draw near, I ask for her help. The answer shows me how much I have to learn of her.

To prepare the innkeeper, I tell him that when the next full moon blooms, I must ritually bathe—alone. I must cleanse my body with water and moonlight together. He does not even ask why. I see the lust as it clouds his eyes. I will make sure it clouds his judgment too. The forbidden and the profane—one sets the seal on the other.

When the moonlight falls into the room and splashes like paint on my body, I light a fire and fill the air with pungent smoke and dreams. I stand naked in the water, letting the light twine itself around my limbs and claim its own.

From another room, the innkeeper watches, his hot blood rising. I can feel it.

The transgression of his eyes leaves a film on my skin that will not wash off. I accept the price and lower myself down into clouds of steam and fragrance.

I look for the fates in the darker corners; I listen for their mocking laughter. It is their move, but they are not here to make it.

The water is hot. Sharply and exquisitely painful.

A breeze sweeps over my breasts; I do not have to pretend to be aroused. Pain is my lover tonight. He lights a fire behind my eyes, and I raise them to the innkeeper's behind the door.

I call him forward with all the strength in my silent eyes. The voluptuous moon and I are a force he cannot fight, and he approaches, as close to submission as a man can be. All I have left to do is resist while I yield, and I will have him—not for long but long enough to find, beneath the thick mass of his hair, a raised scar, a symbol that scorches my hand as I touch it. The smoke of charred flesh loses itself in the silver haze; he freezes, briefly alert.

I press his face to my neck and bite deeply into his shoulder with all my strength. He cries out, I tear the skin on my own breasts with my nails. My blood stains his hands, and he loses himself to me.

I feel what it is to be a man, to conquer, to win.

I look over the innkeeper's powerless shoulders as he struggles for breath and see the symbol, his symbol, burned into the red flower on my hand.

The wound is washed in moonlight, and I feel her gentle cruelty.

I keep the burn on my hand concealed. I wrap both of my palms in strips of cloth and look the innkeeper in the eye when I tell him any wounds I might have are sacred, locked between the moon and myself. He does not like this, but what can he do in truth?

It will eat away at him now. His inside world will begin to crumble around him, undermined by secrets, and fear, and knowledge that cannot be unknown, chasms that open beneath his feet. He has twice the world to be wary in, after all, and this I would not change if I could.

If he cannot reap what he has sown, then let him at least suffer.

In the meantime, I watch him even more relentlessly than I have. His wife and I enjoy his newfound weakness.

When I can be sure I am alone, I study the shape on my hand as it slowly heals. I am patient; I know that a burn takes its own time to heal, and usually, by the time it does, I have learned its mysteries.

But here new flesh does not creep forth from the edges; hollows are left where laid, and edges remain sharp, as if some craftsman fashioned a shape with depth out of nothing and embedded it in my skin.

When I touch it, I feel nothing. It never forms a true scar.

This worries me because every wound, even the deepest, leaves a raised scar. The most powerful tattoo of all, it must be won, not bought. It is not always earned; it always leaves a lesson. And because it is so dear, those who win it need it to show.

On my hand, it has bruised the petals of the red flower stain; blood shows through the skin. I hate it desperately, but it is beautiful in truth. When I gaze at it for a long time in the twilight, it looks meanings at me. They just come, unbidden and unlooked for, in my thoughts.

I close myself into my mind, slowly pulling everything away from my memory of that night that is not part of the actual moment. I have to relive it to do this, it is so hard. Being willingly violated is not something you want to understand or experience more than once.

And when you mix the magical with the mortal, nothing is what it seems.

This much I know: my innkeeper has a scar symbol, a specific and interesting shape, in hard, raised flesh under his thick brown hair, just above and behind his left ear.

I have an indentation of that shape seared into my hand. I am branded.

At no point in time was there anything hot enough to burn between the innkeeper and myself.

Simple enough to know to look outside of the ordinary for any kind of answer. I look to his overlord. Although there is evidence everywhere, I will need to find a connection. I set myself to put the pieces together.

I begin by studying the innkeeper's work. Much is achieved with innuendo, rumor, flattery, and gossip, all the tools of a wordsmith. Where these fail, often, greed will succeed—and lust.

Not many can resist such an array. I am not surprised by his success or the misery it provokes. I cool my face in the wind. It is hard to be patient.

I can see clearly what he does, and I know who tells him to do it. I have no idea how he is told or when.

I need to break him again but a little differently. I tell him I am pregnant with his child and know it is a boy. No man with only three daughters can resist. I begin to act accordingly. I torment him just enough to keep him on edge but not enough to draw unwanted attention from anywhere.

I have been keeping watch at night as long as I can stay awake and alert—and even after that, thanks to Gunn. Patience is almost always rewarded. He begins to unravel.

As his mistress, I become familiar with his routines. He is a man who has never taken night walks, since there are easier ways whose consequences he is safe from. Whether his wife notes the first time he does or not, I cannot say. But I do, and I am ready.

Gunn follows him silently and expertly. I follow Gunn.

Into the woods, whose arms welcome all and whose darkness holds sanctuary for both the sacred and the sick.

The innkeeper walks swiftly deep into the trees. The night is black, but he needs no light. Guided from within, he is safe in this forest on his bent mission.

I am grateful for his strong limbs that break and crush the undergrowth; my way is both easier and quieter for his work. I follow as quickly as I can, until he stops and sinks to the ground. I stay back and try to see what he is doing. He makes it easy when he calls a fire to life on the ground before him. By its light, I see that his hands are trembling as he holds them out over black flames and white embers.

No wood, kindling, flint, or pouch of glowing coal, no smoke and no sound. This fire raises the hair on my neck. I am certain there will be no warmth in it. I find pity for him kneeling and close to shadeless, so far from clean, vibrant life.

I watch his hands, held over flames but not burning. He mumbles words, and on the palm of his left hand, I see forming a small hole, oddly shaped and etched in blood.

I know what comes next. In an instant, I am there behind him. I yank his hair with my right hand and press my left to the scar on his head as he kneels with his hands out and open to his lord's darkness.

It is a perfect fit—searing heat and bitter ice.

Blinding light rips the sky, white flames whirl in with wild winds, screaming and wailing all the voices of hell forever. Then he is there, everywhere at once, around me; I can feel his will, pounding on the door. He is tearing at the walls with long white hands and pitiless strength. He cannot break in; this is not possible for him.

The winds howl out his fury, hammering on my flesh, pulling my hair, sucking at my lips. He twines himself around me; I taste him with my skin. He is so white, so cold, and suddenly so blindingly vulnerable.

I have been holding still, all my strength focused on patterns of white flame and black liquid eyes. I know where to find him.

I am something completely new to him, something beyond his understanding, beyond his endless existence. I wait for him to pause, to think, to catch up.

When he finally slows and the screams fade and the wind loses some of its sting, I use my right hand to toss herbs into the fire. The world reverses.

Chapter 15

I am wet. I am naked. All around me is black; I cannot see. My eyes will not open. I hear strange music, high and haunting, and somehow familiar. It is only in my head.

Around me, the blackness is silent and very cold. I cannot tell if I am here or not. Am I anywhere? Before I can think it, or shiver, warmth floods through me, soaking limbs I don't feel.

He is here with me. He is also naked. I feel him now on my skin, the cool smoothness of a snake and the honest heat of a man. God, I feel him.

He attacks all my senses at once and puts them all under siege. I have no time to breathe, fight, or surrender—or crave. It is done before I do.

I am so thirsty. Small fires are starting everywhere; I cannot stop them. What is wrong with me? I am burning; I am freezing. I suck on his fingers and bite and taste his blood. His blood is real. I feel it, warm on my lips. In my head, the song plays faster and louder, with the thunder of deep drums and hearts pounding.

I scream, and whimper, and beg. I threaten, whip, and cower. I need.

I feel the strings snap as he loses control of them. My eyes fly open.

The world is right again—not a world I have ever seen, though. He is here, sitting beside the bed I am in. Black hair and white skin, terrifyingly real and looking at me with eyes that move like flames, black and alive, and relentlessly lit.

"How like you to play so unfairly," I say.

"You raised no objections at the time," he answers.

I cannot deny it. This angers me and frightens me. I look away. Everything inside me feels desperate. My skin wants to run away. How is he so still?

I see the room we are in. I catch my breath. I want to gasp and cry out my wonder. I hold it, but no doubt he can see it in my eyes, openly mesmerized and asking questions.

It is not a large room, some kind of walls, smooth and forest green. They change and move on their flat surface like living things. But they are not enough. There is a real tree in the corner, alive and growing from the floor—without the sun. Birds sing in its branches; leaves rustle in a breeze I cannot feel.

There is one different wall, made entirely of black stone. It has a deep fireplace full of simple white candles burning brightly. Straight flames at their tips not the slightest dance within them; they defy the windless wind that loves the leaves.

It is a room filled with strange objects, most of which I have never seen and could not identify if I tried. He is by far the strangest. I remember how I can be so sure he is a he, and hot blood sweeps through my skin.

His eyes catch it, and I wait for the man in him to claim his credit. Instead, I see confusion, newborn and wary, before he looks down.

He shifts abruptly in his chair, waves his hand at the doorway, and turns to look me full in the face. His is quite well closed now.

"Who are you? How did you get here, and what do you want?" he asks in a voice he has softened, liquefied almost.

I hear his words, but I also hear that the music has changed. It is the most exquisite sound I have never heard, played on instruments I cannot picture or see, as if you could give actual life to words, and they come as music. I look at him, it gets worse—or better.

He can look as cold as he likes; I know what I am hearing. I have moved him, a god. The god of all that ever matters.

He does not like it. He holds my eyes while three men enter the room, blend themselves into the darkness beyond the circle of light, and begin to play the same music.

Such control. Such distance. Such a liar.

The music in the room now and swelling, stealing into my senses. Falling through me, splashing itself everywhere, mixing me up deliberately.

Where I think myself sovereign, I am just a slave. I rise up, ready to fight, until I see that it is the same for him.

I say, "How do you not know? Since it is your work which brought me here." I marvel that I do not have to explain it.

"I cannot possibly know all that I bring about, and you cannot possibly know anything about what I do at all." He says this with a straight face.

I ignore it. "Where are my clothes?"

He looks away again. "I do not know. I—we may have lost track of them."

I look at him closely, gathering my courage. I get up slowly, wrapping the covers around me, and come to his side.

I touch his skin, on his hand first and then his face. It is exactly as I remember: cold and vitally warm. He has tensed, controlling whatever he thinks he needs to—or not. I cannot tell, nor do I care.

The pulse of my blood is looking for his. Something in him feels it, but he meets my eyes and denies it, staying silent and still.

I look down at his hands. Beautiful, elegant white fingers and perfect nails, but they do not fool me. My skin can hardly forget their strength and precision.

Before he can stop me, I take one of them in between my own. He wants to pull it free, but he does not.

I bring it to my face, gently and slowly. I cannot help it; I bite softly. He closes his eyes, and I feel him melting into me, flooding me. Inside me.

I cry out and leap from the bed; I drop into the darkness of its shadow and curl myself into something small, something safe. But it is no use.

I close my eyes. There is no hiding from the truth.

How can it be that he, who is the source of all my pain, of all pain—how can he be lord of my anything? How does this happen? How in the name of all that is holy did he get in?

I scream this out in my head over and over again with my hands held over my ears, blocking out sound—blocking it all out. *But how? How?*

Through my screaming I hear his quiet, melted voice. "You let me."

It just slaps me. It is already here; he is already here. I freeze. I listen. I feel myself turning, twisting around inside, following it like a river.

I feel my mind opening, with walls falling away, and I can walk out—into him.

There is a long, enormous, and endless hall with doors and doors stretching out in front of me; as far as I can see, there are doors. Something familiar that I have never seen before. I push them open as I go.

I find rooms of all kinds and thoughts, words, and feelings that I knew existed but could never find. I learn secret, hidden things—places in myself I have never been and songs in the wind that we cannot hear. The taste of color.

So many doors, far more than I could ever get to. I open those that call to me.

When there are shadows, I force myself to look in them.

I see new kinds of pain and broken things, wearing their decay like lacework, in dust and cobwebs. I learn that it can be worse to cause pain than to take it. That torture is not always one-sided.

There are doors that remain closed to me, even if I want to see, white and icy and smooth. I push them anyway, and my skin cries out, feeling what I cannot.

My feet carry me swiftly away, running and shedding memories. Finally, I come to a place with no doors. He waits there, standing alone, facing me, and wide open.

I let him see how naked I am, how young. Here and his. He takes it like a blow. How can there be so much he does not know?

He comes in like water, and I am so thirsty.

He goes first to wonder, holding it in his beautiful hands like the most fragile treasure, like it will break at a breath. He stays perfectly still for a long time, as if it is enough.

"Make it storm," I say to him. "Call the winds and the fury."

He does. We reel, and fall, and fly.

He brings the sun after, against the black sky. I watch his eyes widen when I shiver.

How can there be so much he has not felt?

"Once perhaps," he tells me. "It has been a very long time. I have forgotten."

We both know he lies. He was born without innocence. No, he was never born. He has existed, locked in with life he could not live.

He finds the pain in me—the raw flesh of wounds that do not heal. He flinches and turns to look me full in the face. His is wistful. Gently and sadly aware.

This too is new for him. Feelings without definition, beyond empathy, pure and personal. Newborn—remorse and pain for another and living, breathing connection.

He looks to me, the other, and how can I deny him?

It is a dance of doors, windows, eyes, and songs that light fires. Colors blend to make new, imaginary ones that run away quickly; feelings form new words we forget instantly. Rain, twilight, white flesh, and lips that meet with meaning, tongues that touch, souls that twine. Challenges made—something that passes for enough forgiveness. Reasons and things indescribably sweet.

I am drowning in your music. Here you see me as small as I can be; hold me in your hand.

Until you come to the one door in me that will not open for you.

Chapter 16

When I find myself once again in the warm depth of the bed under the tree, I let myself slip down into sleep. What else can I do? The last thought I have is for my body, for the shock it feels at such invasions and how lost it is.

There is no relief in sleep. Dreams come to me—dreams of death where my father falls slowly, without sound, beneath the ax of the Northman. Women's faces twist with pain, and everywhere blood falls from the sky like silent rain.

My father's powerful arms rest on the earth and slowly give up their strength. It hurts so very much that I cannot breathe. I stretch out my hand to touch him, and he is gone; only his blood remains, soaking the dust and screaming for vengeance.

I throw his dust into my hair, rake my nails across my face, and wail the song of women, with its endless story of loss and love.

All that we bring forth death takes away from us.

I sing the song of binding blood for my father and my family, lyrical and eloquent with pain.

He cannot help but hear. He knows the song well, as he knows them all. He writes them. Centuries of sorrow spilling into music that reaches everything it touches. Even this, my dream.

I have heard these songs my whole life; I know them in my bones. Now, for the first time, I see the patterns. I see what we have in common.

I have said he creates pain with no true understanding of it, but he knows it well. My heart aches for him.

I shake myself awake. Clearly, I cannot be trusted to sleep.

The room looks the same, with no windows to let in sun and seasons. What kind of man shuts himself away from light?

The room is not dark; the straight white candles burn on, the same length as when I saw them last. But their flames are deeper colored, their light curiously intense. They cast twilight shadows and bring the same sense of peace.

It becomes a little harder to see. Resolution fades.

No. I cannot have it. I shake him out of my head. What kind of man uses such underhanded weapons?

I wrap myself in a blanket and go look for him. I am not pleased by the continued lack of clothing. Devious, in an obvious way. I expected better from him.

I listen for his music. In my head or not, it will lead me to him—and so it does. I see him through the trees as they shiver and dance, in his hall of no windows.

The gold of sunlight against the black anger of the storm makes brilliant green beds for stars trapped in raindrops. He knows it now, better than I remember it even.

How could something be so complex?

Where art and artifice live with limitless, unforgettable words, and the winds play in him like an instrument. Where the darkest evil wears the face of a child, and innocence becomes harder to define.

Now it is my duty to avenge my family's honor on him—to him, at him, and with him but never under him. In any way.

Too late, in every way.

I find him and get straight to work. "How did you come to be what you are?" I ask him as he stands up to meet me.

He smiles. "Are you not hungry?"

I see it for the deflection it is, but in truth, I am ravenous. Who knows how long I have been wherever I am?

He holds his hand out for me, I take it, and he leads me to a table with food and wine and, across the seat, surprisingly, some sort of dress. I want to feel vindicated, but instead, I am pleased and curiously warmed.

I pick it up and smile at him gratefully and easily—intimately. It is my first and natural reaction. Neither of us expects it, so it hurts us both. The music changes, going sweet, soft, and searching.

I freeze and listen as if I am desperate, feeling the vibrations of strings that are tied to my own breath. Like the music is alive and awake in the room with us and wants to dance.

This time, he finds the wonder on my face, and it catches him by surprise. He is learning how many ways he can reach me.

I cannot believe how much of me is content with such invasion. I could not be more comfortable. My eyes feel as if they have been seeing him all my life. I know his smell and how he tastes, and I have heard his music in my head. Always, it seems, as long as I have breathed.

I drop the sheet and put the dress on, keeping my back toward him as if it makes a difference.

"I assure you I am equally grateful for any view you present, Aela," he says.

Then he drinks wine and watches me eat, which I find intolerable and ill mannered. He accepts none of my subtle suggestions that he should eat something as well, and that the laws of hospitality are clear on this point.

He ignores me completely while silently watching me as if I am a hearth fire or a river—as if I could ever be something to watch in any room that he also in.

Finally, I am sated; I pick up a goblet that has all the colors of light trapped in its crystal walls. His wine is something I have never tasted before and very good.

I drink more than I am comfortable with. This is not where I wish to go; I fight it, finish my glassful, and use its strength to keep my mind closed to him. Then I open the floodgates.

"Why do they call you Lord Pandor? Is it your real name? Who chose it for you? What are you lord of? Where are your lands? Are you a god? What kind of god? Why do you do what you do? How can you do what you do? What is wrong with you? Why do I feel this way? How does any of this happen?" I start to lose my breath and grow dizzy. I stop.

I raise my cold hands to my hot cheeks and look at him mutely. I put all the other questions I have in my eyes and look at him, and hope he has read them all.

He looks away at the end, just for a moment, marshaling his strength, gathering his wits, calling in favors, and composing lies. Who knows what he could do in a single moment?

I do not. I brace myself.

He looks tired before he has begun. He waves his beautiful hand again, vaguely, at the doorway, and men appear; they take away the table and bring out instead a strange, long bench. It is covered entirely in soft black fur and stuffed with down. I sink into one of its corners and curl my legs beneath me. It feels like a nest.

He sits beside me, upright and perfect, with his white hands folded on the blackest fabric. He does not face me. How is there such elegance in such a man? One could never guess at the immense strength beneath.

He looks down at his hands for a long time.

I am watching him. I cannot help but see the change in light as it washes gently over him. Looking up, I see that a tree has grown its branches quietly over us like a canopy, and light dapples through its leaves—sunlight that isn't.

The music is muted and delicate, torturing me subtly, though I am in no way letting him in. I ask him to stop it all and play fair.

"I know that words are not hard for you. Do not pretend otherwise, and spare us both your other efforts."

He laughs out loud. "You can believe me or not, as you choose, but I am unable to control it entirely at this time."

Smiling, he looks me full in the face and makes me see the truth of it in his eyes. I hear it too as the music rises, new strands twisting their way in, weaving and wailing.

I clap my hands to my ears and shake my head, and it is enough to break the threads, even the ones in my head. I am very determined.

"I am happy to help you." I smile. "Talk to me, please."

He has no more tricks to play, so he sighs and then speaks. "Lord Pandor is one of many names that I have. I chose it myself a long time ago. It is a Greek name I chose because it amused me. It belonged to a girl I knew once out in the world, when it was somewhere worth being. I took her name and left her a gift of untold misery. Much like the gift I gave you without knowing you."

He places his hand on my face, the pulse in his blood looking for mine. Finding it and holding it, making sure I cannot run. As if I could.

I have all my defenses up. I am as closed as I can be, but still he whispers in my head, *Stay until the end, Aela, my love.*

I have no idea what that means, but I am ready to, and my reasons are no longer clear.

I listen.

PANDOR

"As I am sure you already know, I am very, very old. You have seen much of where I have been; you know what my mind looks like. You know what I have chosen to keep but not what I have let go. You looked for the child. Did you find him? There never was one. There has never been anything else; I have never been anything else. I have always been as you see me now. How old am I? How can I know, since I was never born the way you were, the way all humans are? I just became. I am.

"Those who made me couldn't be bothered to name me, but it is impossible to introduce yourself as nothing, so I have a collection that I choose from. Pandor is my current favorite. I have names for everything around me, and they change too. It takes a great deal of mental effort to keep them straight in my head. But I do.

"You, Aela, can call me what you like. I have a hundred names for you already, and there will be many more. I have known so many people over centuries of time, Aela, and you are the first to let me in. And you are the only one to ever come in. And now here you are with me. Right here.

"I have no idea how that happens. I cannot imagine why something as perfect as you should arrive in my world like this. You have no idea how rare you are. You are the only one. I know. I have been everywhere at every time. Never have I met something like you. And while I make and unmake the world, I did not make you. I could never have made you. Who did? And why?"

Aela scoffs at this and says, "Whoever takes credit for it, they know that, like everyone, I am deeply flawed. My faults are many, and you know them well. You have seen them yourself, I believe." She makes me smile.

"Your flaws are part of your perfection, Aela. I would not change one of them. I will do my best to provoke them for the joy of learning them. Again and again, as long as I can."

I look away. "Those who made me have not spoken to me for centuries. When they did, it was not something I welcomed. Their actions and their influences are never remotely benign. Always cold, always malicious. I have learned a great deal from them. Empathy is something foreign to them; they have never seen it, do not understand it, loathe it, deny it, and do what they can to destroy it. If they knew half of what my empathy does to me, they would rejoice. I make sure they do not.

"In me, it is the worst kind of sin. They did not put it in me, so they hate it even worse. I do not reflect their best work. I show so clearly their lack of technique, their neglect of details, and their carelessness."

Aela interrupts. "Their skill, however it shows itself." She leans into me and puts her hands on my face. "Their vision, their talent, their creativity."

She traces my lip with her thumb; it hurts. She smells like something I cannot find a name for. She owns me just by being this close. She says, "All the rest is you, and you are the best part."

Things crash all over inside me. "I have told you; the music is not all within my control. Do not touch me if it overwhelms you. Let me answer more questions, and it will calm down. Eventually. If I do not look at you.

"As for my lordship, you will never understand it until you hear the whole. Even then, I doubt you will ever understand enough of me to matter. You think I do not see the shades of your family sleeping in your eyes? I did not have to find you weeping and broken on the ground to know you were. Just let me tell it in the way I choose, Aela, and hear me out to the end, please. When I have done, I will make atonement to your father and your family in whatever way you see fit. Justice for them will rest with you."

She has drawn herself up small. I know what this means. I have seen it before, but this time, I leave her alone. I am in reasonable control of myself, and I have all the time I could ever need.

Perhaps I manipulate the music to some small degree—nothing as obvious as the trees, despite the fact that they are remarkably effective, even when they are apparent, even against myself sometimes.

I decide to let the sun fade naturally, slowly, as it would on a summer evening. That seems to be playing fairly, to the best of my knowledge, since her judgment of such things is entirely arbitrary.

I draw as deep a breath as I can, and it is far too little. In all the long years of my life, I have never encountered something that matters, and all the things that might have are bound up in her somehow, so that she is the most powerful thing—God help me.

She has no idea of it. I have no idea what to do.

She could destroy me in an instant if she wanted to. Perhaps I want her to. It does no good to think all this; the last thing I want is for it to show. I have no choice but to leap. Right off the mountain.

"Aela, do you remember when you woke up this morning? Every morning it is the same, yes? Well, perhaps not this particular morning, but most of them, at any rate. How it takes a few seconds for your mind to catch up with what your eyes see and your ears hear? You remember who you are and where you are, and sometimes you immediately want to forget."

This I understand. I know the kind of traces I leave.

"It is the same for me every single morning, all the way back to the beginning, and that is how I woke that day, the first day. The only difference that thousands of years has made is that I know more. I know very, very much, Aela, more than even you could imagine. I know far too much and far, far more than I want to. Yet I am no closer to knowing how or why I exist, no closer to some way out of here. By *here*, I do not mean here physically, as we both are now in this room. I mean here in every sense except that.

"For a long time, I fought. I asked questions endlessly in my head, where I knew they were listening, back then. The same questions in every way I could think of, over and over, like a mantra that you really mean. The answers were always the same. I knew my business. I knew what they wanted me to do- how, where, and when. But never why. And when I refused to do it, they punished me."

"How?"

"If I say they took away everything, you will look around you and think all of this, but it is much, much more. Much worse. You really wish to know?" Even so, she can never really know. "They took away my senses. One at a time. Yes, all of them."

I cannot let myself even think of it, not for a second. My bones are made of hate. Push it away; don't let—push it out. I am under control now— at this moment.

"Any time you spend in the presence of absolute nothing is too long. Well, in truth, I cannot say nothing; they left me aware of my own existence and aware of time. It was incredibly effective."

Is it still here?

"Sometimes they let a small sliver of light in randomly, without warning, and it was just enough to plant, nurse, and grow the strongest kind of hatred. Living with me in the darkness of the nothing, waiting. So that when they finally let me out, it needed release. So badly. And even when they gave me my reason back, it was unfamiliar, and I was clumsy with it. Clumsy with all my senses, like a greedy drunkard. Insatiable. Sick. I did many things."

"I look at your lovely face, and on mine I let you see what kinds of things, uncensored. A price and a punishment that I deserve. I will give you a moment, my love, to know and then regret knowing.

"For a while, I played games, trying to convince myself that the way I handled things really mattered. That I could have some say in what was forced on me. That something I did or did not do could make a difference somehow. But time moves endlessly onward. In a hurry. On its way nowhere.

"And you have to see—even the blind could see—over and over again that none of it matters. That nothing matters. Years pass, forever. It makes no difference how you measure or divide them or what you call them. I learned that an unlimited supply of anything is far too much. It drives you mad. Very slowly but carefully relentless. And it takes so much energy to feel after a while you simply run out."

I look into her beautiful eyes; clear, uncompromising, unflinching. But so mute.

I tell her the truth.

"I became cruel. I am cruel."

I see her so slightly pulling back a little from me. She has no trouble believing it.

"I have had no reasons not to be and more than enough to bring me here. The worst truth of all, the hardest for me, is you. Already I have seen enough to know that you make my truths lies. You can teach me. I am learning, but I am not sure I want to know. Not sure I deserve to.

"And you, Aela, can never look fully on all that I am, yet you will see enough to send you running away."

Chapter 17

AELA

H e stops talking, his eyes—mercifully—fall from mine, and I let my breath out. I have to breathe a great deal, very fast, and I realize I have been holding my breath for far too long. I lower my forehead to my drawn-up knees, willing him to stop and give me time.

So little to him, so very much to me.

How could he have been the focus of my life for so long and I never see him?

How was it not the first thing I remembered when I thought of him?

How did I have the wits to find him, but not enough to remember that he is a god?

How vast the difference between knowing that some things live forever and touching one.

I try not to remember how much I do know about specific aspects of him.

If I think of that, I will moan and flush; and do all sorts of telltale, stupid things, trapped in my stupid, traitorous body. How do I even begin to understand that?

He lays his hand over my feet; apparently, they were cold, and they love the warmth that floods them. I leave my head down. It is far too much.

My mind has nothing for me—no hidden patterns or remembered wisdom, no real sensations, no control. It feels as if I have run away inside myself.

Soon I can sense the light growing dim around me as night falls. I lift my head slightly to look; it is dark, and I am alone.

My feet are still warm, covered under a fur now. Overhead he has brought the stars of home; by their light, I see that he has left me the wine.

I drink it.

My hands are curiously white; I can see them quite clearly, lit with life in the darkness. They know what they want. They are luminous with it.

I trace the symbols on my palm with my fingers like a blind person would. I close my eyes and try to think. I will say that I trust him, but I am very, very careful what I think about.

Truthfully, I have no reason to trust him, given who he is, but I have seen for myself how little real weaponry he has.

He is no kind of warrior, but he is definitely a man.

His words thud painfully back into my mind: *They took away my senses.*

Until now I had believed that only death could do such a thing. I struggle to imagine what that would be like, a life without life. I can hardly bear to think of it. And for how long?

Gytha would say he chooses his lies carefully. I know he tells the truth; I have seen the scars.

I sit up. The room takes its time following.

I curse the wine, which has won, and try to hold the world still with my hands. It does no good; I am the one spinning.

How do I know that I am not still, in fact, in there? Where in the name of all that is holy am I? How did I get here?

Where is my world, my dog, my life?

I shake my head wildly, slap my own face, and bite my lip until it bleeds—anything to stop my thoughts and not think of Hemwyth.

Too late, his name is in my head, the door is open, and he sees.

I slam it shut. *Please, please do not ask me,* I beg him in every way I can. I cheat, implore, and lie. I sell myself.

He is cruel. He calls it forth against my will with merciless strength and clear, unrepentant eyes.

I have no choice, so I will tell him. I will try not to hurt him.

Somewhere, a small part of me will never forgive him.

But I can play his game with his rules. I take his own music, bring it into my head, and play for him. I use his own notes to speak to that part of him that only he understands.

Somehow, in my head, there is a whisper. *Sell it to him. Force it on him. Do what you have to do. Say whatever it takes to keep him from lighting his infernal fires. Keep him as far away as possible, as far as you can convince him.*

The sound I call sweeps down the side of a mountain, riding the wind and demanding to be felt. The muse flies through and paints the skies, and her words rise up.

"This is Hemwyth. He is a fighter. That much of him is as you made him. Like every other warrior called to the song of your war drums. You might dismiss him. What are physical strength and precision but two of many kinds of discipline? They can be mastered, you will say. And you will be right, but you will be so very wrong too."

He smiles. "Who is he?"

I call on a different muse and the words of ancient bards and start strong. "'The Song of Hemwyth,' as men will sing it, begins with a young boy trying to understand that he will never see his mother again. That there are demons his father could not save them from. Lust and greed and the worst kind of betrayal. Things I believe you are acquainted with, my lord of lies and half-truths."

I draw him pictures, call images to life with his winds, and keep the music living. I hold his eyes, mine as blank and bleak as he has made them, and I show him what it looks like from the other side, where the sharp scent of blood is personal.

I show him the inside of wounds. I show him the view from his arrow tip; his blade; and his honorless, meaningless trophies. All his dealers of death leave swathes to be read—patterns in the blood and the dust, songs in the wind.

The brutal, beautiful rain. *His* rain. It soaks him. Right through his cold skin. Looking for a heart to kill.

He feels, through me, the pain of losing. Every widow, every mother, all of them want to be heard, and he is listening. He is *feeling*.

I have unleashed wide and wild things that cannot be contained; I have no control of them. He has no control of them.

There is no way to hide how I feel about Hemwyth. Nothing he will not see. I can watch it as it writes itself across his face. This will never do. I find strength from somewhere; I have no idea where.

I start to sing again and take us back to the story. "He sits, pale with shock. How can he trust a face that brings this kind of news?

"And when the face of trust itself, forged in bonds of blood and memory, shows itself to be false, what then do you trust? Nothing. You can trust nothing and no one."

Who am I talking about? I stop.

Gods above, how do I make sense of two very real, completely different worlds? I look at him, sitting so carefully motionless and mute, on the end of our soft, forgiving bench. So straight. So correct.

I try to explain what he must surely know—how the effects of his work vary. How they burned through Hemwyth, leaving unseen, unsung scars. Yet he grew so carefully that nothing can bend him.

"Not even you," he says, running his fingers down my cheek.

Another truth I will hate, followed closely by the one that almost kills me. There he sits, familiar with all of it, knowing all of it.

There I see, suddenly, the same scars and the same horrific pain. The tremendous difference—every kind of difference, the one that tells.

I see the truth. Bold and naked and right here.

The truth that Hemwyth is not what matters now. The truth that everything, all of it, revolves around him. Pandor. His name, current or otherwise, sings itself into my mind. He is already here.

I cannot think of Hemwyth, cannot even call him into my mind, as hard as I try. Horrifying. How can I? What is wrong with me?

I try so very hard. I scream for him, and I am screaming for him.

I blame him. And hate him. And love him. And hate myself.

I have to fight. I must fight somehow. "What kind of earth or gods gave birth to something they could never love? How can there be life without a mother and a father?

"What sort of god submits to another so willingly? Without recourse to justice of some sort? What kind of world is this? Where is this? Whoever heard of a powerless god? What kind of god are you?

"Gods have names!"

I say this to him, mean, so mean, like I never knew I had in me.

Not a flinch. He just sits there, inhuman and immune. Many kinds of mute.

It makes me so angry.

"Can you say something? Can you find words for me? Can there be something that makes sense?"

It hurts almost unbearably to think of it. I do not want to be in this world. In *his* world.

I go blind and perhaps mad and hit out at him. I hit him as hard as I can, over and over. He does not move.

I slap his face so hard my hand burns. Then the rest of me catches fire.

I pull my hand away. Drums pound in my head, harder and faster. In the walls around me now, drumming my heartbeat. I look down at the scar on my hand; it throbs with white heat, white pain, made from my own blood.

What can I say, when this is how it is written? When my body chooses sides?

I find his naked skin and love it like I do. He plays his music with my body.

I surrender.

"I want to see," I say to him. We have finished what we were occupied with. His face is pressed into my breasts, cool and hot at the same time. It almost looks as if he has color in him. His hands are tangled in my hair; his limbs are tangled in mine, so white. He is so white, and yet still we look as we should, entwined, with no doubting who is the man. It confuses me and begins to arouse me. *No, I need to focus.*

He hasn't moved. He remains the same temperature, but music is coming now—strange, wary-sounding notes, ethereal and almost discordant.

"What do you mean?" he asks quietly.

I wiggle my way out from under him, find a blanket, and wrap it around myself. He lies there, his beautiful black hair falling soft, so softly across his perfect face. His black eyes look at me with forever in them, and I forget what I was saying.

What is wrong with me? Always! I mentally slap myself, like I slapped him—hard so it hurts.

"I want you to tell me how it works. How you work. In my world that you torment and here in your world. In your house, if you like. Perhaps you should start with that. Tell me what this world is. And then, before you tell me all the rest, let me watch you work. Show me everything you can. I need to see it all."

I have his attention now. He slowly sits up. He leans against the wall, then turns to face me. "That is not a good idea, Aela, not at all. You did say you would let me tell it my own way. Let me, my love."

God, he is so beautiful. So very odd, and so perfect. I cannot even tell you if he has the muscles of a man. The hidden strength that cannot be hidden. I don't care. I feel everything I need to feel. All I see when I look at his body is a perfect match for mine. And mine starts calling. Demanding.

It is exhausting, keeping my thoughts in order. I look at him intently. He knows what I mean. He takes his own blanket.

"Please," I say, "stay out of my head. Please let this be simple and clean. Just be honest with me. Deal honestly with me. I am trusting you. I do trust you."

"I'm glad." He smiles. "Once, out in the world a long time ago, I learned that it is a good idea never to let a woman be hungry. Certainly never talk about anything important with a hungry woman."

I cannot help but laugh out loud. *Too many kinds of charm. All in one place.*

He rises gracefully—there is no other word for it; drops the blanket; and walks to the door. He turns to look at me. "You will find clothing in the trunk under your tree. Wash, dress, do whatever you like, then come to me, and we will eat. Then I will tell you whatever you want."

Quite a remarkable and easy victory for me. It is hard to trust him. I am so hungry.

Oh God, a bath. I want a hot bath. Here come the men with the copper tub and buckets. *Is that lavender? Evil, evil man.*

When I am clean and warm, hair washed, toweled, and loose to help it dry, I put on the clothing I have chosen. I try not to think about how well they fit. How does that happen? And how they feel...

It is almost impossible to resist soft slippers, so I do not even try. As I put them on, I hear the first notes of new music. The sweetest, most innocent kind of music. Like a child in a man's voice, irresistible, with the seductive naïveté of the newborn. A voice like a kiss.

Although I know very well he is working his arts, I follow. There is something here I have not heard before.

The closer I get to him, the louder the music becomes, more and more intense, until by the time I see him, it is falling on me like rain, with every part of me in drought. I walk straight to him and kiss his perfect lips, tasting and feeling and wanting to pin it into forever.

For a long, long time, he makes love to me with just music and taste. God help me, it is more than enough.

He knows even this. He lowers me gently into a chair just before my legs give way beneath me. The music ebbs, becoming something that can be borne.

I watch him walk around the table, like always, dressed in black and mystery.

He sits silently and watches me eat. He knows how I feel about it. I may or may not fling something at his head. He drives me mad. Eventually it occurs to me that he is enjoying himself, and I calm down, then ignore him entirely. This is the most perfect bread, hot and fresh, and it has my attention.

I look around us, seeing what he has brought to distract me. From the obviously devious perpetual twilight to the abundance of birds. He is brilliant.

Our table sits in a corner beside a stone hearth. The fire is alive, warm, and snapping. The walls fade into the shadows of dusk and then somehow become forest, dense and growing darker as the light fades.

Inside is outside; warm is cool. His face holds both promise and threat.

The music is rising now, stealing in like mist and winding itself around me. I am overcome by how much I love him. I let him see it, I *will* him to see it, in as many ways as he can.

Then I put both of my hands on the table and look him full in the eyes. The music falls away and night comes to enfold us in our circle of flickering light. Everything around us goes black, blending into nothing but infinite darkness. How can he know me so well?

"How do you do this?" I ask.

"Where is *this*?"

Chapter 18

PANDOR

" 1 n truth, I cannot tell you, Aela, since I do not know myself. I have done my best not to know for as long as I can remember. From the little I have seen, I must assume I am somewhere far to the north, where it is cold and dark forever. With no light, no seasons, no warmth. Not quite nowhere or nothing but very much like it. The only part I took to was the ceaseless wind, with its endless, empty promise of somewhere else.

"I kept it and brought it here in my head, where I live. It whispered in my ear and told me I could make this anything I wanted. I felt some kind of hope then. I marveled like any child and saw something that wasn't there, and even then, I forgave it for the lie. It did not need to be true; it only needed to be different. And so it is. I change it when I want to, and often, it changes itself, meeting my mood before I do, but always, ultimately, under my control.

"And when the world was interesting, I would go out. Like you do when you pass through a doorway, I went out of my mind and into your world.

"For the first time, I felt the different pains of a corporeal being. I smiled then and for centuries after at such pitiful, paltry pain. Of course I did. Let me give you a metaphor for the pain I feel, one that you will have some idea of.

"Think of it as a long, difficult birthing—of the soul and the heart and, often, the mind. As if you could command specific, different kinds of pain for all of someone's being, all the different parts of him. Fully *customized* pain. Uniquely and eternally mine. And it would be the pain of a fatal childbirth. Endlessly bleeding out, and it never ends because nothing can ever be born through me. I cannot—I could never—bring forth anything worth having. Anything of value. Anything innocent.

"Then you come along and show me that someone somewhere can. Something priceless. Unique. And apparently without motive."

She is so very simply beautiful—like a thought from a clean mind, like a real smile. I try to remember what I was saying.

"I willed myself in and out, and to amuse myself, I chose a different door every time and, often, a different name. Not always the same me even. Just at random as and where it fell. A different place, different time; a surprise for me, if you like, despite having caused much of what I encountered.

"I played how I liked, with another set of rules crafted for my own benefit and bent to my advantage. I learned much that I did not know; I was taught much that I had made up. I took many souvenirs, not all of them offered. I am a collector, I confess, of the finest things dreamed up by the best of your minds.

"You will have seen this when you looked and watched, silent and transfixed. Like everyone in every time and like me every time. I would be happy to tell you about them…

"Ah, I see you want me to stick to topic. Very well.

"Let me summarize what I have told you so far. For reasons we cannot fathom and dare not try, we find ourselves together here in my world, which, as far as I can tell, is or should be inside my head. I cannot confirm this, of course, by any means. I have no proof either way. You know as much as I. You are here, you can touch me, and I can touch you.

"No, do not worry—I will not. Please grant me a degree of self-possession. But if you make me speak against my will, you cannot expect me to be gracious about it. Ah! What—"

She has slapped me again, a bit hard for my liking. I am more of a giver than a receiver that way. I take a moment to reflect on the joys of corporeal punishment. But she is serious, looking at me.

"I understand you, Aela. Leave it now. I feel it."

I take her hand and press it to my face. Where we touch, life springs forth. How is this possible? I feel it here inside me, inside all the parts of me that matter.

"But what is this? How is this? How do they let this be? There are traces; there must be traces somewhere of some kind. Ah, Aela, this is a fear I never imagined I would ever feel. You are a fear I never, ever could have dreamed of."

She mutters something about spouting kettles. Who in hell could ever understand her?

"I will go mad. I am going mad, surrounded by unseen traps and the worst kind of dangers—yes, lovely thing, I see the irony. And the beauty and the wonder of unseen things again. The possibilities and the pain. I see it all. I can deal with it all, but I must be the one to pay.

"I do not know how to make it so."

Some instinct tells me I must keep distance between us, but since when have I had instincts? Must I play it safe? If so, nothing will work better than to tell her the truth. I know it. I loathe it. Why can I not just keep her? Like the rest of them? Oh, there are many ways to lock things. I want her so badly. I need her. I will give up all the rest. There goes the music—it even tortures me. How can it be?

Heaven and hell, which do not exist—here now. At the same time.

"Aela, when I look at you, I see real, actual love—how trivial a word for such a thing—for the very first time. The kind they sing about. Something I have sworn does not exist. For centuries, I have sworn—I have known—that there was no such truth. And here you are, waking up a heart I never knew I had.

"Let me tell you then about me.

"A long, long time ago—thousands and thousands of years—I was made. From some sort of malignant, foul, loathsome substance. Who knows? It does not matter. I was made, and I was locked into a room with walls of darkness and left there.

"And that was all for a long time. As much as I can guess. It was far too long to waste effort trying to remember.

"But then I became aware. Suddenly. Completely. For the first time.

"My mind was a newborn thing; it did what all newborns do, but I was not. I rested, already old and listless, crouched in the shadows, while my mind cavorted and sniffed and leaped aimlessly around. Insanely clueless, totally unprepared. For anything.

"Even if I had conceived of such things as ugly and evil, nothing could prepare me for what fell from a black sky without warning. A sudden wash of flame, like liquid, boiling pain, flooding down on me, not missing a corner. Every intimate place. I could not even scream, like I knew it was useless and nowhere near enough. It burned out my heart, and I turned black with pain.

"After a while, I could feel it flowing down through me, and I watched from my impaled mind as it pooled around my feet. Then I felt for the first time my own body, as it is here. Irretrievably scarred, devoid of all warmth but here physically and spiritually—a mistake that vexed them greatly—and present of mind. All grown up. And if I had ever a memory of such a thing as play, it was pitifully easy to vanquish. A puff of smoke over a smokeless fire.

"The fire lives in me; the black flames are as much me as I am. I can never exist without them, but I can control them. I keep them locked in a circle, in a room with walls of darkness, and that is where I do what I was put here to do.

"Through them, I see your world, Aela. And I make my decisions.

"Please, my love. Please let me take you somewhere else. Just for a while. We can come back as soon as you want to. I promise."

Thank goodness for the eternal ambiguity of words. I have brought in the singer for the last while; I watch her curl into something softer. Then I can see her starting to breathe a little faster; this must be harnessed and brought in. I call in something strange, something so beyond different that it will drive her crazy trying to understand it. Ah, I have her attention now, in a very different way.

"Come with me, woman with sunlight trapped in your skin. We will go into a place where the walls are made of wind, so no sound escapes them. You will see and hear something that could never be seen anywhere else. Something that does not really exist, but it is here. I will tell you about it.

"As you have seen, Aela—or, rather, heard—there is a part of me that can only express itself with sound. I can be the worst, most horrific sound you will ever hear, but mostly, I choose not to. At least I choose not to use pain for words, because one day far into the future, when I was scavenging, let us say, I came upon the finest, most universal language that has ever been. The finest that ever will be.

"It is a kind of music made on instruments that are beyond understanding, even by me. The most eloquent, lyrical, ethereal, and sometimes even brutal music. And there is a man whose voice speaks for every person who hears it. Like real, clean, true magic. It just shows up, and wherever you hear it, it fits. He fits. So beautifully."

This is amply demonstrated by his voice, which comes in and takes over mine. Right now. I let him since he is far more expressive than I could ever be.

As soon as we hear him and his musical magicians they own us; I cannot help but stand still. Listening, feeling, and succumbing. After a while, when I am able, I start again and hope she can follow me.

"It is as if what he sings becomes some kind of law. I myself, not the least articulate person, cannot bear to hear myself speak. Until I have

91

mastered the perfection of his every breath, of words and sounds as they should be spoken, as they must. He is setting my own standards for me, and I do not measure up. And not just in the world of words, my words.

"Even when he is tired or less than content, the changes in his voice are simply a new kind of charming, a new type of enchantment."

I smile, although this is far from the time for it. "You have already heard his voice many times over as you hear it now. He sings every strong emotion I feel, one way or another. Well, he and his wondrous flock of musicians. I took them and brought them here—all of them."

I stop outside the doors. She needs to know one thing first, but so many others will follow. She has not a hope in any hell of coming to grips with it the first time in. All I can do is try again.

"In this room are many men and some women who all speak different languages but still understand one another perfectly. Yes, it is a large room, as large as they ever want it. They understand me, and I them, but you will not understand them all. You will understand a few, and they will surprise and, possibly, dismay you."

Nice. At least now I get the true meaning of words like *blithering idiot.* But how do I explain this? I want to explain it in such a way that I do not come off looking so very evil. I know that the end justifies the means, but can I get her to believe it? Try again.

"As I mentioned before, I am a collector of a very select group of things. The one quality they have in common is that they move me in some way. Any way. In this case, I am speaking of the man whose voice somehow became mine. Here in my own world, in my own head, in my spirit. He was able to find his way here, or perhaps it is his voice only. I do not care. It found its way in. Like you did. But not quite."

I cannot stop my hand; it finds her face, and I trace the outline of her jaw. The curves of her lips etch themselves into my skin. They burn into my mind, something I will never forget. How could I? I force myself to go on, walking into the distance I am making between us.

"I followed the voice as soon as I heard it. It had found its way back to me from a place that is over a thousand years away from you and your world. Like an actual miracle. With no smoke, no tricks, no lies. Far into the future, these men weaved the notes that rang all the way back through time, as far back as there were ears to hear and souls to need.

"Once I understood this new language, I saw its patterns and light, its particular hues and tones. Written into songs that transcend time, that *were never ruled by it* ever. I found them everywhere, in so many places, once

I could see and hear and feel them. Yet they are incredibly rare. Once I could touch them, they could—and did—touch me. I do not have to tell you what impact they had on my own existence.

"Someone, at some point, gave it all a name—not me for once—and it is a ludicrous thing. A mortal insult if such a thing does exist. Like it could be captured in one word. It came to be known as art. It might have stood for something longer but equally meaningless. I do not know or care.

"Such sounds and visions—and life, linked only by their impossible genius—could never be circumscribed by definitions or labels, just as they are not subject to time. In truth, there are no words that could justly name such a concept. You simply know it when you encounter it. When you are gifted with it. It will own you. It already does."

Her hand in mine feels like a trusting bird. Warm and alive.

"Let us go in and see them at work or otherwise; it is as they decide. What you must remember is that they will not see us or hear us when we go in. We will hear what we choose to. Fine, yes, we will hear what I choose. Trust me, frustrating woman. You will not be sorry." Does she really imagine she can keep me honest? "We can walk among them; we can worship, you might say. We can wonder at such impossible beings sprung from the mud of the worst world I could make for them."

When I turn the handle, I understand very clearly the risks I am taking here. She will admit of no reason for keeping anything caged that longs to be free—so far.

Yet surely the results—the sweeping, overwhelming, madly and maddeningly intense things that you feel when you listen to it. See it. Touch it. All of it. Surely, they are worth any price?

"Look at the compensations." *This is true.* "Eternal, never-ending adulation, they will hear it from parts of the world they have never heard of, in languages they will, magically, understand. Their ancestors will hear them and all their children's children's children. Their reach will expand into forever; audiences will adore them and worship at their feet. They already do."

She looks at me as if I am witless.

"Well, ah, I am speaking of the many solid reasons for the contents of this room."

I open the door.

Chapter 19

AELA

H e is talking. I hear him, but I have no idea what he is saying. I am listening to the voice. Where is it coming from? It is inside me. Is it mine? I want it to be mine, but I have never sounded like this.

I do not understand this music, but it understands me.

When he opens the door, it pulls me in with strong arms and sets me down, breathless and rapt, at the feet of a group of players. I look up and see everything else that is in this world.

There is music all around me, all different kinds, all at the same time—tangled, tortured sound. There are players of every stripe that ever came across a threshold and bards, minstrels, ancient poets, virtuosi, visionaries, magicians—even some madmen. There are simple saints, and craftsmen, and something that looks very much like an angel.

There are instruments whose graceful lines I recognize and others whose ugliness disappears with the first note. Mesmerizing. Calling with the siren strings of sound and lust, and deity. I will lose here. When I turn around, he is gone.

Oh, he is playing games with me. He must be. Curse him. Curse you, wherever you are. I am ready for some new words.

Ruthless, relentless tides, sweeping me into new sands and new shapes, laying bare to the winds things that are best left unseen. *Get out of my head.*

I admit it; I might be perhaps somewhat enamored—yes, fine, obsessed—with this theme, apparently with reason. And he is here again, pulling me to my feet and making me touch him.

A huge room. I never see the end of it, and once I am inside it, the sounds of the winds are lost, and it does not take long for me to forget them.

But the music is like the air of this place. It is everywhere, unseen but alive in every other sense possible, including some I have never felt before. He places his hands gently around my face just as it overwhelms me, and it is all silenced.

"I am sorry," he says, and when he kisses me, a new song starts, just one, quiet, eloquent, and exquisitely timed. Even as I know this, I cannot bring myself to care.

The walls of wind keep the music within here; nothing can be heard— nothing can be wasted—beyond these walls. Unless, of course, *he* wants it to.

He starts to talk a little faster. He waves his arms about with something like energy. I am astonished. Is that a flush on his face? He does not stand still for a second. He has closed the doors behind us, and they disappear, sucked away by the wind, soundlessly.

We walk around and among this gathering of rarities. He makes Herculean—and here is a new word—attempts to justify all of it. He breaks my heart; he cannot even maintain the thread of the conversation—*his* conversation.

He comes to a sudden stop. Of course, I walk into him. "Ah!" I recoil. Physical contact of any kind is never a good idea, but my God, he smells so good.

He gets quite strange now. "Look to the corner," he says as he makes one. "There, under that tree—that is him. You can look at him. I never do. I never have."

How odd to find an adolescent alive and kicking in one so *old*...

His voice is hushed. I have to lean to hear him. "I watch him all the time, and I listen to him, but I do not look into his face, and I should think the reasons will be immediately apparent to you."

This baffles me. I will have to think. Later.

I strain my eyes looking, trying to see the face of the voice. I cannot. Whoever, *whatever* he is, he is surrounded by the dappled light of trees, like a living mask. He has been granted the gift of privacy in the middle of this battlefield. He and his.

All the fire, trees, and magic will never make this anything but a battlefield, or a prison.

It looks as if they have been given everything a man or woman could ever desire, far beyond mere freedom from want. I see statues and waterfalls, starry skies and strange lights that dance in the north, old stone and ancient trees. Wolves slip through the woods, and danger lingers like a scent. Water plays in immortal rivers. All the things that live forever and speak to those who can hear.

We keep walking; my mind goes numb with the effort to absorb. I have no hope of understanding.

He, considerate host that he is, has kept control of what we hear. He likes to say he "curated our experience," but we both know better. He is filling my mind as carefully as he can.

Then the voice and the music changes …

It is strange—unpleasant almost—but I am drawn to it as we all are by the color of death. It is disturbing, and I am not sure I want to hear it. I look at him. What is he doing?

It shocks me through to my bones when I see that he is hearing it for the first time. He is rigid, perfectly upright, but somehow leaning into the song. Like facing full into the wind. I can see him hear it with his skin.

The sounds go on for so long, stranger and stronger, so that when the singer comes in, his voice is timid and wavering, lost in the rhythm. Hanging thin in the air but persistent. I have heard it before. *So much to say and so many ways to say it. Always a new lesson.*

I see him singing, he is fascinating—impossibly strong, intensely alive, fearless. What else could you fit in such an unlikely package? I remember his voice—feeding me, playing on my skin, terrifying me, saving me.

Then I listen to the words. Is he mad? I am horrified. Is he really saying what I think he is?

Ah, I can see why Pandor looks stricken. And sick. And very quietly, terrifyingly angry. No, anger is not the word. It is the quietest, sanest, softest rage.

I draw my breath in sharply. He turns to me, and he is someone else. Something else.

Oh God, run!

The walls explode outward, far out into blackness, and suddenly, we are alone. He stands facing me with so much to read in his face that I grow dizzy. It changes nothing. I am afraid.

The music rages wildly, all the winds at once screaming to be heard.

And then, quite brutally, it is back to *him*, he says, "Did you hear them? Do you see them? So many, and still, there are those who hide. Only their words come out. It is the kind of underhanded tactic I might admire if it were not so very personal.

"And all of these men and women have exclusive access to a realm or world that I cannot find, and I have looked."

Yes, he is definitely flushed.

"How do I know? I do not have to see it to know it is exists. And there they can meet and share stories and secrets and mysteries and magic. They can pass their puny judgments with impunity. They have their own fire, and no one can see it without their consent. I cannot see it. Fire is *mine*."

Now there is something new in his voice. Something I cannot like.

Somehow, he knows. It disappears, replaced by something quite righteous. And blind.

And irresistible. He is every kind of magician.

"They are free to write songs with outlandish names and even worse constructs—inane, quite hurtful, ridiculous. Songs that criticize me or my work boldly to my face."

He is astonished at such flagrant disregard for boundaries. Such brazen disrespect. He even looks hurt. Around us, the walls close in. We are surrounded again by trees and firelight and musicians. Sounds weave like smoke, swirling and rising, relentless and wild, utterly untamed.

"What does something like "There, There, (The Boney King of Nowhere)" even mean? I have heard it; I am forced to love it. Yes, even though I feel the slap every time I listen. Like they have something to teach me.

"Without even thinking of things like trespassing or violat—things like infringement, I can object to their combining talents, efforts, and knowledge in attempts to hurt me or to leave. By any means, devious, ruthless, and even cruel—whatever it takes to set them free. They cause me a considerable amount of work and inconvenience."

God in heaven, a frown appears on his face, plain, simple, and instantly familiar. Familiarly human.

I interrupt him, choking down the obvious, and ask, "Does that mean there is a point when they might succeed?"

"Look around you," he says. "Look at them, some of them playing for us even though they cannot see us. Somehow, they sense something different. They must sense you, my love. Can you hear how wildly they play? I cannot stop them. Ah, Aela, you are in danger, I tell you. And it will do you no good to run, even if there were somewhere to go. You will find yourself a slave to many masters."

He stops. He cleans the lines of his face until they are cold, and then he walks on. The music falls and dies. It is in mourning now. I can see on faces the willing resignation of those with no hope.

But the song says something else.

We come to a great hearth, a circle of stone for an immense, hot, glorious fire. It smells like fire. The sap of a spruce tree, primal scent of comfort; every man knows it. It snaps and threatens and blesses those who brave it, who sit in its circle of light. I stop abruptly. I hear a voice I know.

And there he is, bent body but straight, true voice. The voice of stories. He is singing the songs of my people. The songs of his people, who were *my* people—songs I have never heard. I hear their voices crying out into the skies; he wails their pain into his.

His voice calls me like a command, and I go to him.

He sees me.

I take his hands and squeeze them, the lifeline to something else. Some kind of relief floods through me, and some kind of regret. And perhaps a shiver.

I ask, "How is it that you are here, Wistan? How then did you sing the songs of men in the halls at night? Not so long ago in a very different place?"

I am reeling; my head aches. I cannot keep up with him. I look around for him, but he is gone again. Like the coward he is. Ah, I need to understand something! Anything that makes any kind of sense.

I fall to my knees; a circle of hands surrounds me, a circle of bards, and minstrels, and magicians, all around me.

They want my story. I should have known it.

Only Wistan can have it. He already knows a great deal more than I, I think. He will not hear mine until he has shared his.

He says, "What is there to tell? You know him. Can you not imagine? Can you not see clearly what is written and why?"

"No, there is nothing clear about him."

"Sit, my child," he says, and waves his thin arm like a wand. The flames hiss out and rise to the rafters of wind above us. "What you see around you is his Hall of Music. It is but one hall of many. We are always free to visit the others; you might even say we are encouraged to. He keeps the most marvelous things, Aela. I cannot begin to think of words for them...

"All of us are here to play and make more music always. We come from different places, different times; some ancient, some that will not be for a thousand years."

It hurts me that I believe and understand this most outrageous of claims.

"You recognize our group, and we you, because we came from the same world. The same place in time. He brought us here, but from the look of him, I will wager that he did not see this coming."

His hand shakes as he brushes the hair from my cheek. It is my father's hand. "How you come to be here I cannot guess. You must tell us. But first, I will try to help you understand here, where you find yourself."

He raises his eyes, looking over my head, beyond me. Behind me. "Outside this circle of light, you see the others, but they cannot see you. Do they turn their heads as you walk by?" He smiles. "They would.

"This much I can tell, and so I know you will not reach them. You can watch them light their magic fire circles and dance. You will see the muses hiding in the songs of the night; you will witness the miracle of birth. But you can never see them clearly, nor hear them, and they will never see you. He thinks it safer that way."

I turn my head quickly, but all I see is the trace of light *he* leaves behind. Branded on the wall of wind into which he vanishes. The back of his head. I am not surprised. I turn to Wistan.

"I *can* hear them if he says so, Wistan. I heard them on my way to here. I hear them. Do not tell me that I cannot. And I do understand everything he said. I feel it. But this? How? How can you be content to stay captive? Tell me, please. Tell me how it was to be brought here against your will."

He gives me a glass of wine, his wine, and while it lulls me to somewhere safe and soft, Wistan tells me his story.

"When you sing the deeds of great men in their own halls, you earn some of their glory as well as their wealth. And you leave a part of yourself there in their hall, so when you sing of them later, you will always be singing of home.

"I sang of you, lovely, living Aela, and your beautiful sister and noble father. I cried aloud and sang for your spirit, trapped in your eyes as flames engulfed you. How was I to know it was not so? When I stood in ashes long cold and listened to the earth telling me the story. All were gone, and so I must write again a dark dirge. One that broke my heart.

"One that he heard.

"He came to find me, a new friend along the bench on the wall. A new patron. The most genuine and generous one we have ever known, all of us. We live the luxurious lives of the wealthy, which true artists rarely attain. Jealous men are happy to keep them starving. But he knows what to value. What to own."

I watch his hands as he polishes the curves of his lute like a lover, then coaxes her to sing for us.

"He brings us here all together, where we can share our souls and our songs. We must make music, whether we will it or not.

"But here it is, Aela. This is the thing for us. *He* can command the *Muses*. Who could ever imagine such a thing? But it is so. They are here for us always. A never-ending gift, we can call them whenever we want to. True, they do not always appear, but then they come when you have not called them, so it is never predictable. It is as certain as they are trapped. Like us. For us.

"What one of us could resist such an unholy, miraculous collaboration?

"But he is demanding. Only our finest work, wringing notes from the winds, the skies, and the storms, finding words for the vivid life of time and space. And not mere words; he needs meanings, truths, ugly or heartbreaking. He understands betrayal; he wants it enshrined in music that no one could resist. He wants to hurt, but he also wants to love the pain.

"And we give it all to him because not one of us would miss such a chance, this chance, that brings us here together.

"So I can weave the haunting notes of the future into my tales of heroes, and far into the future, they can listen to the stories I tell by the fire. So my words will find their way forever onward through the furthest reaches of time. And the ancients can weep when they hear the new world created by new music. Music as clear as the stars themselves, with endless resonance. Life of our own design.

"It is a kind of power—I admit it frankly, as we all do—and one we cannot do without now we have held it. The power to move others. Even him. The power to change things.

"And he makes liars of us all when we let ourselves come, drawn by the same sirens as every man who journeys. I have heard them."

There is no doubt of it. I read the wonder in his eyes. For a moment, I understand the jealous.

"And we stay. As far from those who love us as we could be. We will write their songs of loss, and he will use them. And those who never knew us will know us now forever. Some it will torment; others it will transform. We will be reaching, we *are* reaching, everything."

He looks up at me from his stool. His face is wistful, confused, and resigned. "When he wants it so, though. Only when he wants it so."

This makes me so angry. "So he just keeps you here? For how long? God in heaven, how long, Wistan?" I thump on his remarkably firm back, so frustrated.

He smiles. "How would we know?"

"Anyway, none of it makes sense. You must be wrong, mistaken or misled. I heard you sing in halls not so long ago. I cried like all the rest. I felt your connection with the past as you brought it to life for us. *You were there.* "It follows that you have not been here long; we must make him let you go. Go back to wherever you were taken from. Go back, and sing the truth, as you always have."

I am determined; I am ready to win at any cost. I will find him and make him.

Wistan shakes his head at me. I do know why he remains here, and he knows that I know.

He puts his lute down, stands, and pulls himself upright. "I have not aged a day since I came here, and I never will. None of us will ever age as long as we are here. None of us knows what would happen to us if we went back, or forward, to our own time. We have asked him many times, but he always maintains that he does not know himself."

He looks at me, twisting his mouth into something like a smile. It is no stretch for either of us to believe otherwise. He lies as easily as others breathe.

"It does not matter, Aela, for I would not go. Let my shadow walk the long roads and shelter in high halls. He sings well enough, and one day he will die. His body will return to the dust, a corporeal death for a corporeal shadow. My shade will come home to me here when that happens, and my words will find new meanings."

I stand and stare at him, more confused than I was before. The fight has gone out of me now, but the need to remains. Every nerve in my body is exhausted and exhilarated, very raw and very aware. I turn around slowly, and then I walk away.

I call out to *him*; I look for him in hidden corners of my own mind. I cry out for him with all the love I have for him. And the anger. I listen for his voice here in his Hall of Music. I look for the doors, walking along the walls for such a long time.

I do not find them. I grow weary of walking, calling, and listening as hard as I can.

Finally, I lean back against the wall of wind. I do not care what will happen to me if I do. I am tired. And very cross. I fall backward into his arms as he catches me.

He turns me around and presses his lips to mine, really the only way to silence me. He is kissing himself into me, and I hear his voice in my head.

Give me a chance, strong woman, let me show you something before you make up your rules and judge me. Close your eyes," he says, and picks me up like a child in his arms. "Keep them closed."

Sounds start to change; his footsteps are lost in a vast silence, wide and cool on my skin. I feel him sink to the ground and open my eyes. He leans us back against a tree and closes the black sky around us, bringing it closer and warming it up.

His hands hold my head; he looks at me with his face so close to mine. His eyes ask me questions that his lips will not form. He turns my head and tells me to look down.

I see, below us and some distance away, a scene veiled in mist and mystery.

There are players, like slim black candles, faces lit and casting away darkness. I cannot see them clearly, but as they begin to meld with their instruments, the creative force within them takes flight and catches fire. They play a song that I can see as well as hear feel as well as know. It flows over me with a force that is physical.

It is here, alive. They are here, alive, and the music is everywhere. I do not understand their language, but I understand their song.

Here is where I will struggle. I will wait for words that can encompass it, but they will have to be made.

PANDOR

She will wait for a very long time. I have tried and failed.

I close my eyes and ask as simply as I can for the song I want her to hear now, in this way, at this time.

It begins. And that is the last of my control.

She sits and stares, instantly arrested by the novelty. I cannot blame her. It is so very different. Countless times I listen, and each time, it takes me by surprise.

I do not understand his words; it is as I wish it. I will never allow myself to understand them, unless he forces it on me. So they can mean anything, and often, they will mean whatever I want to hear.

But when he wants me to know something, I will know it. He will find a way for me to know it like nothing else, and I do. Every time. One might look at us and wonder who holds the power.

The same song, but never the same thing twice. Always a pure, visceral response, when the simple, corporeal sensations are more than enough. Even I do not have to find anything else. But there will always be something.

I watch her watching them. I see the slow, inevitable capture of her spirit. The hounds are coming. She turns to look at me, and her eyes are helpless. Like the rest of her.

I understand.

Can you hear that, Aela? Almost, I could believe in something noble. As if there were such a thing as honor. And that these impossible, remarkable men have touched it.

The song builds, almost unbearably. Ruthlessly and shamelessly taking control of the rest of—both of us. A pleasure defined by its pain. By the wounds.

He sings his soul into the sky until he sees her, bloodless and trembling, as vulnerable as only he can make her. He stops. The music stops. He lets her go, like he lets them all. He does not like to own. He is a fool.

In the silence, I feel how exhausted I am. Such a thing has never happened to me. I look down to him. He is standing still, as helpless as his own power makes him. He looks to me for a moment like a man.

But in the end, it proves most effective. All of it, all of them. Written across my face, drawing blood. The helpless blood of weakness, of involuntary atonement.

I kiss her beautiful face. She wipes something from the side of my eye and sucks it off the tip of her finger. I freeze this moment before it changes. I send everything away except us.

Around us, the luminous walls of a warm hut appear. The bed rises soft beneath her. I want to quench the fires within us that he lit and left. I am too tired.

I kiss her again, so sorry. And then I fade away from her.

Part 2

Chapter 20

Do you like her? I made her myself. I look over at them—three of them—sitting there like gaunt, frozen idiots. Three faces, each one different, each one, technically, interesting—some of my best work on noses, definitely. Craggy, misshapen, noble. I love a good nose—but all of them are wearing the most perfect, stupid expression. Perfectly blank. Like they are not listening to some of the most exquisite sounds that exist anywhere. Did you think I would do without?

Admittedly, I have never had them here together, all three of them, seated (my manners are impeccable) and with this excellent fire. And her. Are they deaf? And blind? And broken? If I could be aroused, I would be, but there is no excuse for them. Do they think something like this just happens?

She is *right there*. As perfect as I could make her, and I am the kind of artist whom every artist I have ever found would give his life to be. I am a master plagiarist. The very best and—quixotically—also the worst.

Do I seem like the kind of imbecile who would collect the finest of 'creatives'—isn't that a lovely word—and not 'lift' from them? You can say what you like about the inevitable, tragic destruction of eloquent languages—our work, of course—but their modern manifestations can be quite concise.

I, however, have no need to be, as you are a captive audience. I may obfuscate and fulminate, and vacillate, and lie, and soliloquize, and make up words at my liberty. And use the word 'and' in whatever way I like. It is fortunate for you that I have a natural distaste for lengthy, tortured sentences. See?

I will employ them when and how I choose, and you should hope that you are a quick learner.

Certainly, the three morons sitting across from me are not. I cannot understand them.

She sings, at this moment, the line "They are dead," proving that she at least is not—for the moment.

Allow me to enlighten you.

Among the creatures under my employ, there are some I have taken more care with, where I exerted some effort even, like these three men before me. The first one—I call him Achilles—is fashioned after an ancient Greek, an enhanced version, if you like, since I took the workings of several and combined them into this beautiful, golden, perfectly formed young man. He can fight like his namesake, think like both his contemporaries and his descendants, dance like a boy from Knossos, drink like a well-known demigod, and argue like—well, take your pick. So, I definitely do not understand his impassive face at this moment. But I shall move on and return to him later, since he obviously needs time to marshal his arguments, assuming he will have any for me this evening. As I intensify my gaze, I see a bead of sweat form itself on his temple. Interesting. I like it. Let him squirm, since he is obviously broken.

The second man is a different specimen entirely. I call him Genghis— you might get the idea, and you will likely guess where I found him; certainly, I took something like that. But as remarkable as the original was, he could be trying at times, and his manners were deplorable, so I put in the most exquisite Asian jewel of a geisha that a country as interesting as Japan could create. A little Confucius, most of Sun Tzu, and enough of Mao to discomfit him. Just to make it balanced, I chose a girl, at random, from a bizarre race that arises at some point in time in a place known as Southern California.

But since I am forced to look at him for lengths at a time as he argues passionately, lucidly, and insanely for whatever item is on offer at the time, since I wanted to *like* looking at him, I put it all in a perfect package that I stole from another place in the same time. A lot of interesting stuff in some parts of, well, you might say the future. It is all the same for me, but I found him in a place called England, lovely name for a fascinating place, but he was laboring under an impossibly *cumbersome* name, so I imagine he was pleased to leave it behind. Isn't he beautiful? I let him bring most of himself with, well, us, I guess. Look, I do not have to explain it to you. Or understand it myself.

At any rate, for reasons I will not go into, I think of him as Sherlock, and I expect him to act like it, but I suspect the girl was a mistake. At any

107

rate, he sits there, chewing something carefully that he never seems to finish or swallow. And like the other two, not a thing to say.

I admit his melting impassivity (does anyone do 'still' as well as he does?), a perfect setting for his magnificent mind, is as magical on me as it is on women. And pretty much everything that looks at him.

I know she is looking at him from under her perfect lashes. Are all women bitches?

I will remind her that I am the one who made her, and I am as good at unmaking as I am at putting together. I must remind her. After this song.

And the third man? He is staring at the fire, like I am not even in the room. It is an infection here in my room, in my world, this indifference to me. First her and then Cesare. Handsome, mesmerizing collection of all that is finest Italian.

I would squish him like the proverbial bug he is if he weren't actually the most brilliant. He is likely composing music for the stupid fire while he watches it, and I will love it. So I leave him alone, even though he is the most likely to appreciate the kind of beauty I have created here in her.

He can wait. Let me tell you about her. She is the most beautiful thing I could make—the most beautiful thing I have ever made. I would have hoped you would understand that much about me; it is not all hell and horror. Again, I remind you I am the original aesthete.

So let us take unlimited means and materials as a given. What would you expect me to create? And in case you forgot, dexterity, unscrupulouslessness—perfect for me is it not? You know it. Wanton plagiarism, voyeurism, sexism, extortionism, charmism—sweet juxtaposition, yes? There aren't many 'isms' that I have not mastered. Or made up. So I gave her a selection—even I do not know which ones. I like to forget.

I said you should keep your wits sharpened. Keep up with me.

What did you think I would create? I was not born yesterday (double pun there). I started with music, unlimited composability—isn't that a nice, precise word for it? Just one preset, and it can be changed, but it is set for now to encourage the minor keys to come forth and dominate since it best represents—something I do not need to tell you.

So, as you know, I have an excellent collection of musicians. I borrowed from some very interesting creators, but I gave her a voice that was just an idea in my mind. I waded deliberately into the pain I feel for Aela. My lovely, impossible Aela. Without wincing, closing my eyes, or shrinking into my skin, I let myself feel it. I embraced it. I made love to it. And then I made it sing, sing the melting and the dying, and the only real truths I have ever known. I captured all of it and made her voice from it. Can you hear it?

Do not ask me why. She tortures me with it.

She sings now about fuel and fire, and every one of us knows it differently. I stare into the real fire, here in front of me, and remember other fires.

For longer than I care to admit. To you.

But there is never any real doubt.

I stare this fire down. I keep it fixed in my eye and pull the life from it. It curls itself downward and dwindles and dies in a long, slow moment. Without smoke or warning. Finally, Cesare raises his eyes to mine.

What should be the best, finest mind I have made (he is a Borgia). You have his name; think of what went into him. He is modeled after his handsome namesake but—yes, you guessed it—an improved version. His wit and energy and fatal fascination, at the peak of his powers, just before his world began to bleed. The sins of the flesh leave their traces (I flatter myself), but it is not something I have to see...

Think of the other names you know. My favorite, Michelangelo, and his marvelous, brilliant contemporaries—that sort of thing, so many at one time—all in the same place—it does not happen often, thank goodness. Remarkably inconvenient for us, a lot of 'overtime' fixing a mess like that. But it was a wonderful place to be. I stayed for a long time, and when I left, the best came with me.

Once in a while, you throw up a—what do I call it? A ruckus? A rebellion? A stupid, futile, valiant, insane, forlorn hope. We have to do damage control, and I get to go hunting.

I have said elsewhere (who knows if you will read it) that true genius never meets itself. It is not entirely true.

The universe, or what I know of it (or them, however you like it), does not allow genii to connect, just as it allegedly does not tolerate vacuums or flourishing stupidity.

Unfortunately, although I am excellent at everything—trust me, it is worse than it sounds—I am not so good at following rules.

Who do you think came up with the phrase, nicely embraced by your lot, "what they do not know will not hurt them?"

So, I certainly play fast and loose with whatever I can, whenever I can. I threw a great deal of it into this man.

You have a word for what I call the Party of (that) Millennium. I think it is *renaissance* or something like it. You could do better, I am certain, but your sense of drama is skewed. It was an astonishing time, without doubt. As I said, my minions were scrambling, but I found some wonderful 'stuff,' and made this poor excuse for company in front of me.

This wretch whose eyes defy me without reason. I am seeing strength in him that I did not put there. I have the uneasy sense that it would not be so easy to cow this man. I imagine it never was. This does not please me either. I scowl and consume a remarkable amount of wine in an attempt to make it up to myself.

He sits there, literally made from the finest materials (think David. I knew him, and yes, he was), marvelous creativity to steal and exploit, from the Circles of Hell (quite flattering, actually) to the kind of wits that paired words with weapons successfully. Can you imagine? See if you can spot Lady Macbeth in one of these worthies; I am a fan. But for some reason, great passion for the visual or other arts (I hate this word, as you know, but I use it so that you can picture it how you need to in your small, pathetic way) precludes other, very important passions. As if they could not cope with more, great artists have very limited understanding of love.

I have had limited, painful exposure to it myself, but that is another story.

I did not want my quasi-Italian to be passionless where it counts the most. *Is it even possible?* I wanted more, so I coaxed a lovely, properly sensual friend of mine to slip in from an island in the ancient blue of the Aegean. I see her there as she stretches like a well-satisfied cat licking the cream from her lips in the depths of his eyes.

I have an idea why she is so pleased. Her counterpart, the mirror image of what is not seen in the smooth, handsome face of Cesare, she is playing the piano and looking out promises from under her lashes at *him* too. He is looking back, all that Italian passion on intimate display. Am I *flushing?*

They are brave, these two. Or is it three?

There are threads here that I did not weave. This is, after all, my web.

I say, "She is not here for your pleasure, my friend. She is here for you to see how well she is made, how well *I* made her."

I snap my fingers, and the music stops (I love this). I stand up slowly and walk over to her, sitting before the piano (this is one of my favorites because it responds to the right musician), and I stop behind her.

The lighting is perfect. Can you doubt it? Fire and candlelight play on the lovely alabaster of her neck. Do you see the swan? Do you see the flush of winds on her smooth, priceless cheeks? I was trying for moonlight, but since I have not seen it for so long, I cannot be sure it is right. Another story; you must remind me one day.

I caught enough sunlight for her hair, though. Blonde will be my new favorite if I have any say in it. I like it piled on her head like this, carefully carelessly; she does it to please me. It allows your eye to follow the gentle line of her brow down the curves of her neck. Look, you can see her pulse, just there in that hollow ...

I make the mistake of touching her. She is cold; there is no blood beneath her skin. And even though I know this, it makes me shiver. Never touch them.

Back to my chair, my glass, and a man who finally has something to say. I dare him to with my eyes.

"She is only dead to you, the same way I am only dead to you." His eyes move deliberately away to her and back to me. "My lord."

Perhaps he wants me to squash him like the bug he is. I would if he were not correct.

They are dead. They are the best I can do, but they are all dead in the ways that matter.

She sits with her hands folded on her skirts, spine straight with simple strength and grace—everything that is lovely in a woman: candlelight on slopes and shadows in valleys, mystery, and things I will never know. She is the same as Aela, after all. Even if she is dead.

I feel her draw away from me the slightest bit. Her hands lift like wings, and she begins to play a song I have never heard before. It is breathtakingly, achingly, desperately beautiful. Listen. I defy you to find words for her lovely, fragile, incredible voice. From it, I learn that his name is not Cesare but Dorian.

I freeze myself, hands already on their way to something I prefer not to know, and make myself pick up the bottle and fill a glass of wine for him.

Although this has never happened, not once in many, many years—only Achilles is allowed to drink, since the other two misbehave in ways I do not appreciate when they do—he reaches for the glass, and I feel his fingers brush mine. Are they just a tiny bit warm? He takes the glass and puts it to his lips without hesitation, and he does not hide his appreciation for the vintage.

I am as amused as I am annoyed. He can be grateful that my sense of humor is still so healthy at this point in my existence.

I am nothing if not pragmatic when something beyond my control flings itself into my ordered life and literally fucks things up, in every possible way that can happen, since I am subject to whatever the hell is happening in my world at this time, with no hope of understanding it and in fact quite helpless, which is not a word usually associated with myself, if this is the case despite the fact that none of it is actually possible; despite my murky origins or because of them, nothing has come so far that I cannot handle, apart from Aela, and she is still pretty much taken care of. No, that is the wrong phrase. What I mean is that she is still where I left her, despite what you may have heard to the contrary. Well, since my words are tripping themselves and this is all rot, I might as well 'just go with it.'

"Ask me some questions, Dorian. I might answer a few of them. I like you and your newly minted sources of testosterone."

He laughs out loud, and that alone almost makes *me* laugh. I wish I remembered how. He is a brave man.

Technically, he is an evolving man. I am interested.

I look over at the vision in the pool of candlelight. She plays on like a living ghost. Her fingers dance with what looks very much like life. Really, my work is in a class of its own.

"What is her name?" The first question he asks me.

I am genuinely sorry he has asked. "She does not have one."

The music plays on, the same melody, but it does not sing the same. I make her change the song.

Genghis and Achilles both stand up abruptly, bow in my direction, and walk out of the room. Genghis, as foolish as he is brave, turns back and looks at Dorian. "Ask him about the fires."

This does not please me.

But he asks it anyway, so I will tell him—now, in front of her, and she can learn from some of the very best how to speak for the voiceless.

Chapter 21

H e wants to know; no doubt all the rest of them want to know. I could just show them...

The truth is that there is so much, they have no idea. Think of what you know about me.

I will tell him about the fires. He will be sorry he asked. You will be sorry.

It is something I have no problem admitting to. If you want details, I can assure you it is quite simple. It happens like this.

My work does not require my constant presence to proceed. I have trained enough of you to do much of it for me, and those who are here are the finest of their kind.

They came of their own volition, alchemists, masters, kings... searching endlessly for something like me. They gave me the most charming names. My current favorite? Beelzebub, just for the way it feels when you say it. Try it the next time your lips are frozen. Rituals, games, clumsy, naive attempts to woo me. Highly amusing. How could I resist? I would be a fool not to put their considerable skills to their best use.

I think we have established that I am not so much a fool.

Alchemy is a marvelous tool. It turns base men into monsters.

But even the most talented still lack imagination. So when I am in certain moods or something has displeased me, I go to my room of fire, and I play.

Therapy, you might call it.

And sometimes I am inspired by things like music, or pain, or intense, eroding frustration. I go and unleash my hounds. I rain lightning into the world, and blood gets splashed and colors everything gloriously, like a different kind of storm. Men use words like *rivers of blood*, but you must see one to truly understand what it means. It is so very beautiful. Think of fresh pomegranate juice on stained glass between you and a blinding sun. That is one of my favorite metaphors, and I am always very fond of metaphors.

A song comes into my head at this moment, suddenly, just like that. Pushing out what I am actually hearing, somehow. "Decks Dark" and it immediately throws me off topic. Righteous vengeance, creative discipline, malign energy—all these wane away, and I am left again, unpleasantly reminded that there are increasing numbers of things beyond my control.

She stops playing, rises like a sigh, and moves out of the candlelight. The room grows colder.

I shake myself mentally and light the kind of fire that goes with the song they are making me listen to.

Let me just say that I have been intimate with my own forms of torture—from both sides (more on that later). I in no way desire more. And when a woman just drives you mad, and your situation becomes increasingly unbearable, your *world* becomes your torture. And when all other stands are against you (not that you care) you break. I did break, and in so doing, I broke many other things.

Nothing falls alone.

They have made me vulnerable. Aela made me vulnerable. When I hurt, everything hurts.

It is nothing for me to call, as I did, into the world and the winds for everything that fears and, that is fearful. That is afraid of the dark. I call for them to find every Aela in their world, their village, and their lives. Find them, and burn them.

But not my Aela. She is safe behind the walls.

Now they bring "Desert Island Disk" and hope their honesty and bravery will move me. It works well enough to be its own worst enemy. I take "Ful Stop" and put it on repeat loudly enough to make the leaves fall.

Not my Aela, just every other one, in every age, anywhere.

It looked like a rain of flames out of the black sky, flying down and lighting immense, wild, and dangerous fires. I *love fire*. Conflagration. A pathetic word for that kind of fire. I must think of a new one, for seas and oceans of it.

Do you remember? Fueled on fear and hatred, there is unlimited supply. It thrives in your kind. You are wretchedly easy to wreck.

How could I not hold healers in contempt? Like small, pathetic, defenseless, fluffy (there is no other word for it) things. Made of light and just as weightless. They are ridiculously simple to use and to violate. They are all made of moonlight, every last endless one—moonlight and futile, fruitless, irresponsible, unforgivable hope.

Nuisances into perpetuity, I can tell you for certain. Millions of them, urged into rebellion by their mother, the moon, the greatest bitch of them all. Shocking language—forgive me—but she and I do not exactly see eye to eye. I cannot even be bothered to think of proper words for her. She is nothing.

Let me tell you about her.

I am likely the only entity, let us say, that has ever seen her, well, au naturel. As you can imagine, she is indescribably, breathtakingly, astonishingly beautiful. Even I cannot look at her directly—well, not for more than a few moments at a time. And so, I do, well, actually, I did, to be exact. Looked at her. More than once. Until she saw me seeing her.

I am no stranger to pain, as I have mentioned, but the scars from that particular encounter are a different kind. Never healed, always insanely sensitive, itching endlessly.

As long as I have been alive—a long time, ad infinitum—I have never seen a woman or man that beautiful. I do not have the words; there are none. I cannot help you form the picture in your mind. Your imagination will be grossly inadequate. You must deal with it. How can I even trust my own memory about her? I have not seen her for such a very, very long time. I thought I had no memories, even of her.

And there she is, shining out of Aela's skin. I hate her. She lives in Aela. And Aela lives in her. It is the way it happens. It is the way it has happened.

How did I not see this coming?

And now that I have, I see traces everywhere. Unmistakable. I must have been blind.

As I remember it, she shut herself away from me. It was only long after, a very long time after, that I ever closed myself to her. And so she has been absent for all these centuries. I have lived without her shadows for so, so long only to find her here in Aela, who has come and conquered.

And she shines out of every healer like her, every woman who troubles to search—those gifted with sight and senses too strong to be contained in the pitiful, weak corporeal prisons they inhabit. Ah. What a mess. A simple, incredibly complicated mess.

I believe it has been mentioned somewhere the nature of my occupation.

We are the authors of every kind of misery, knocking you down; you fall so easily…but this is complicated.

I have asked myself why. Over and over, in every language. It makes sense in none. Why does she allow them to be so tortured? What kind of goddess is she? Why does she not protect them? Why does she not fight for them? I throw them down. I grind them into the dust and take their lives with their blood—, and their children when I want to. Did you have any doubt? Did you think my hands were too clean for it? (My grooming is impeccable always.)

Some of the best and most finely focused minds have carefully *created worlds* for women. They are handcrafted by masters. Men so devoted to their work that they choose to live in the squalid, infested holes of the worst places we can make, just to watch their work carve itself into their victims.

They consider themselves artists; they can be found in strange places, writing themselves into story lines.

But they leave the carnage on the field. No gentlemen in that congress, no subtlety, no finesse, no style. Just the stench of death.

Women face the most horrific odds. They are not all of our making, the horrors. Sometimes things grow out of our control. (Not my control. As I have said, I am rarely there.)

Some kind of defect. I cannot be bothered to understand it; things get together and recombine themselves into new, unknown, unknowable, and unstoppable forces.

Women suffer.

Men suffer too, of course, if we are doing our work properly, but it is different. Men always have a hand in their suffering. A stake of some kind—challenges, chances, a role for them to play. If they play it well, if they are good at the game, others suffer, not them.

And we know who makes the rules.

But women have it forced on them; they never see it coming. They are betrayed by their own bodies and their own natures. Our work is always top quality. But she, the moon, she could help them. They are her own; she should help them.

It hurts to find them. Always rising up from whatever hell we fashion for them. We admire them as much as we need them to suffer. How could we not? We revere them; I worship at least one of them.

But when they hurt us, we fight back. I fight back.

I have always fought her, the moon goddess. I hate her, I fear her, I love her. I will always love her. I will destroy her in the end.

Somewhere far into the future, a bard will be able to claim that burning witches light his way.

116

I let that little slice of hell waft through Dorian's ears just to wake him up. Just to show him I am finished speaking.

He is staring at her ghost, standing in the corner, wavering in and out of sight like a breath. Still a gift in the shadows of my fire.

"Do not distress yourself," I tell him. "She is not far, and no doubt she will return to torment me when she chooses. It will be interesting to see how she occupies herself in the meantime."

I say this in the most careful, gentle voice; only the hairs on the back of his neck catch the minute, delicate, lacelike notes of menace I gift him with.

His eyes turn to me. They are Viking blue in his Italian face and even stronger than they were the last time I looked into them this closely.

"May I have more wine, my lord?" he asks and waits for my answer. Not as brave as he looks perhaps. But I know better by now than to expect things to work the way they were intended, to be what they seem, or to make any sense at all. I fill his glass and brace myself.

"Most of us understand that it is your pleasure to keep the deeds of one hand from the other, so to speak. We also recognize how well you do this— you are not the only one with means—but by now we can usually see what we need to see and know what we want to know. If we want to know it."

He is smart enough to know that this will have occurred to me, so he does not hesitate to say something that inflammatory. This begins to get interesting.

He says, "As much as we are all eager, quite truthfully, to listen to you tell stories—and they are always fascinating and fascinatingly vague—I am, at this time, looking for specifics."

Now I am listening.

I know what the question will be before he asks it. The real question is, do I answer it?

"What happened, my lord?"

I hear his voice, quiet and sane and interested. His face, handsome and holding everything I know him to be, is open.

Is there no end to the malfunctions here?

That face, with that beautiful, graceful voice, to me, here and at this time—Achilles would be proud. That face deserves to know. But God in heaven, it is not something I want to think about.

In what feels remarkably like punishing myself, I let myself remember.

Chapter 22

There is a young man standing in front of me. I cannot say whether I have seen him before. I have better uses for my mind than the storage of something like him.

At any rate, I can see that he is quite agitated. This is something I have never experienced. I wouldn't have imagined that there could be someone so, well, what other word would you like? Foolish, it is. Someone so lacking in judgment as to have any type of emotion at all, never mind letting me see it. I am quite ... nonplussed—that is the term for it. A wonderful word that describes the incredulous, naive wonder of a bear who feels himself being poked.

Emotion is not an asset in my employ, I assure you. What could possess a man, disorder his wits, strip out his instinct for survival, and let him just open like that. Very vulnerable.

Because I know that both of us know this, I am quite disturbed as I look at this messenger. Whatever ill wind he carries will hurt me worse than I will hurt him.

I am quite nauseous, in truth—something I haven't felt since Rome, really, except for the occasional consequences of overindulgence, which even I must helplessly endure. That is a completely different story.

I will find the original owner of the phrase "Do not kill the messenger" and punish him.

If I could, I would kill this one before I hear what he has to say. He is terrified. As am I.

Half of me, newly awakened and insanely inconvenient, pities him. The other half, the professional half, sees a victim—a justified victim.

I must make myself listen to what he has to say. He tries. He cannot find words. His gestures fail him; his body betrays itself. I have nothing but contempt for him. Who is he, and how does such a thing come to be here in my employ and in front of me now?

I am not accustomed to this sort of dialogue. This halting, trembling, wet-looking presentation in particular is entirely new, and let me just say that I have had enough of the novel.

If I were the kind to do such a thing, I would spit on him. He can count himself lucky that my manners are faultless and that he is still in the condition he arrived in. Let us hope he remains that way.

He stammers. I am almost amused, but really, I have no patience with this. I tell him either he can find the means to convey whatever it is, or I will rip it from him, and he can be sure I will pick the easiest way in.

Before I go on, let me assure you that this hapless messenger will not suffer unduly. The worst that will happen to him will be close confinement for a short while.

Ah, I don't even know how to do this. Do I let him tell his pathetic story in his own pathetic words? No, I will suffer enough. Let me tell it to you in my own way. Let us pretend I am telling you a story, like a bard would—and no doubt will one day, if any are left alive.

Well, a more concise, modern bard, I flatter myself.

Everyone knows the prequel. It will be lore somewhere at some time. When gods and mortals collide, it is never quiet or dim. Gods love to walk among you, hidden in various guises: handsome, well-fed peasant; perfectly manicured ruffian; cunning snake—you get the idea. Some encounters are powerfully destructive; others light the heavens, and mortals learn things they should not know. Fireworks, hurricanes, evil tides, and miracles. It all happens. And, as you know, we occasionally, or even obsessively, collect.

The finest souvenirs are lost in the mists of time and find their way, well, here, mostly. I cannot speak about the collections of others, and I cannot pretend to care at this moment.

Except that in this story, everything is upside down. The heroine pretty much battles her way into the hero's world and just takes over. Trust me—that is not how the stories go. I know; I write the originals.

I find myself personally affected in unforeseen ways that seem to invent themselves at light speed. For example, as I tell you this, the music suddenly floods into my head, *he* dares to sing to me now, bringing "How to Disappear Completely," knowing full well that he will want to desperately very soon, and will be unable to.

Without doubt, he is the cheekiest human being I have encountered, and I have met Aela.

"This is too much, I am afraid," I say out loud to the vision and to the fire and the man, and the music stops. I will not listen to him right now.

I stop talking, but he is in my head; *they* are in my head. It is all in my head. How much did I drink?

Aela, how could you do this to me?

Aela, my goddess, my love, my life.

As I scream this into the darkness that is my mind and soul, and core, he is singing: "Everything I touch turns to stone." In my head, I cannot keep him out. The song is "Blow Out." He knows it is coming. He knows that I know what he has done—what he and my beautiful, my precious, my mine—*my Aela* have done—and he will know what I have done.

Snow and wind and fire and hell and cold and pain and despair and want and violence and horror—all these things are coming for them, coming for you, just as they play it. Hear it for yourself. Think of what will happen while the sounds and the winds roar, and I bring the rains.

And when it is coldest and darkest, evil will set out on long missions, like it always does. Death is the worst in winter. Everything that should never happen, I make it all now, in my mind as I remember this.

In my worlds, I will be careful. Nothing must be damaged that will leave a mark that shows. And, most importantly, nothing must impair their abilities. They will need to describe it, to share it.

And so brilliant, soul-searing eloquence will follow one day, after wounds have healed, and what remains can try to grow.

Suffering will produce the beauty it always does.

But everywhere it will be winter.

Because a thin, tortured man with a mind of gold and a heart of poison needed to say something to me. He is not content with the 'lessons' he gives me when I listen to him; apparently, I am not to enjoy the learning process. Have I mentioned that I am the teacher?

Or because a beautiful, wanton, wild, and irresistible woman who might have had a broken heart, might have been suffering, who was born suffering, had enough of suffering and wanted to teach me her own lesson. She might have been more moved than she could help, I do not know how or why what happened happened.

And to make sure I cannot blame her, he brings "Four-Minute Warning," and I am reminded yet again that this is a man to be reckoned with. A mind, a soul, and a force to be reckoned with. And he does not come alone.

If he can rule even me sometimes, how can I blame her?

But even as I listen, the temperature inside me is falling and falling. When I am cold, it is cold everywhere. Winter is one of the simplest means to raise the wrong kinds of hell; it requires almost no effort from me. But this time, I am not in control. I am afraid of my own hurt and my own anger.

He sings that he will blame it on a "Black Star". I can produce those.

He is trying to control me with his words right now; I am distracted until I think of him with her. He sings so appropriately that this— it is killing me. What songs did he give her? What did he say? What turned her away from me and toward him? I will find out.

Do not try to blame it on her confinement. She is there for her safety; do not forget it.

I think carefully. What have I heard? A song about doors—that will terrify her and make her angry. Ah, it could have been "Spectre." There is nothing that song would not fuck up.

But we all know it will be "Burn the Witch." He brings it now to remind me. You see the kind of man I have to deal with.

I am very good at burning witches. I have been known to do it personally, on occasion, simply for the amusement of such a farce. Sometimes I attend those I am not responsible for as well.

They burn in every way, in every time. He has captured it perfectly. I was incredibly inspired by this song; it makes a perfect background now, mingling with the smoke and helping it to sting.

That will be his punishment. I will make him watch. I will watch myself as we burn and burn. Every Aela but the one who matters.

Many things will perish in this kind of cold and this kind of fire. That too can be laid at his door, at their door.

Aela, my love, why would you do this?

You know that once I have started, it will be very hard to stop. It will ignite like a match to gunpowder, and then it will grow into an endless, eternal riot. Few things I can create have the power of a mob. That is all you, your kind. I did not make it up, since I had no need to.

Aela, tell me it was not what I am afraid it was. Tell me you were furious; tell me how hurt you were. I know that I hurt you.

It is his fault, all their fault, weaving impossible tangles around her, around me, wielding powers I did not give them, owning their own mastery. Can you hear them, you insane man, as they scream?

Who did you think I am? What did you think? Did you think?

Aela, my love, you did not give me enough time. I could have—I am blank here. Even now, I have no idea what to do. He brings "Codex," so exquisitely appropriate. So, what I am feeling? What can I do about him?

I close my eyes and listen, as you should.

I try very hard to be there, but I think of his hands on her, his mouth, his heart, his insane heart pounding against her beautiful skin. How many ways did he touch her? I can only imagine.

I go and look for a Frenchman and his "Chapter 19."

Chapter 23

When I open my eyes, Dorian is still sitting there, trying to keep his face from betraying his—I want to use the word *pity*, but that would be somewhere even he would not dare to go. He does well, my baby Medici. I like him even more for it.

If only he could control his—well, his ability to control himself. It is unforgivably discourteous; offensive; ill advised; ill judged; ill received, I assure you; and irredeemably rude.

But I am quite confident that he is sorry that he asked. This pleases me, and I pour him another glass. I think I might even call for some good bread and meat. Men seem to like that sort of thing when they are drinking.

The music has changed. I was not aware that I had changed it.

Can you wonder why I keep them? Still? Then you have not listened. By the same immutable law that governs all the things I cannot control, universal reason states simply—for the moment—that if you do not listen, you do not deserve to hear. So you never will.

I, Pandor, add further to this. I have said it before: for those who do listen, it is a fatal decision, and it is the last one you will ever make, as far as they are concerned. After that, the choice will be taken from you. All it needs is for you to let it in once, and you will be possessed, let us say.

Everything that finds its way into you becomes you. It is a mutual agreement between you and what you have let in. Others have said it better than I—quite a few others, in fact. More than I am comfortable admitting to.

By telling you this, I have let you in. Or you will believe that I have. With me, it is not always easy to tell.

But you need have no doubts that they are in me, that I am, in more ways than I can stand myself, infected. The audacity of this astonishes me. Their audacity. His audacity.

He knows. He knows I cannot really punish him without punishing myself. Watching witches burn is child's play— even children watch— without punishing myself, and I am loath to do such a thing. Not that I do not enjoy certain types of punishment, but I am more of an inflictor that way, so for me to submit, well, you understand. It must be very, very special for me to let something hurt me—to let in words and magic and whatever kind of insane sorcery is responsible for things like them. And the others, and Aela.

I seem to have become even more—as impossible as this is—vulnerable. I did not see this coming.

This does not reflect well on me, considering I can see and go into both the past and the future. And other places. Technically speaking.

I look up at Dorian with different eyes. He puts his glass down and leaves the room. The last bit of warmth goes with him somehow, even with the fire still burning. I curse him, the fire, and the mad musicians who document my life.

Who mess up *my life*—however they like.

It is complicated and no doubt beyond your comprehension. I will not submit you to the details. But I certainly need to sit very still, alone, and think. I need to consider it.

I need to understand it.

Listening to them is like listening to the sound of my existence. My long, long, grim and sordid life. An unknown inception, obscured by the blackest clouds of the starkest pain.

All kinds of hell in the centuries since. The worst symphony in history.

If you have not realized it or sussed it out yet—why are you all (you know who you are) so fond of such an expression?—I will spell it out for you in black and white so any idiot could understand it. Wherever you are, whoever you are, I, or something of mine, will have reached you. Think of the worst pain in your life, your deepest, most rabid fears. They will have been put there, especially for you.

Humans are fond of inventing deities who can be appealed to in times of loss and fear and hopelessness (thank you). You will entreat the gods to spare you; you will cast stones and read signs invent your silver linings and look for meaning. You will find it everywhere.

Like a treasure hunt, bits of light in the dark morass of your world. We let you find them. They are scattered everywhere. How else could you see the darkness that surrounds you?

Pain is always most effective when it is administered sporadically and alternated with periods of light. With pleasure.

It is like he is in my head even when I have shut him out. I swear it. He is singing "Scatterbrain" now. Exactly the kind of pleasure I am speaking of. And remembering.

Now there are no escaping thoughts of Aela. She comes flooding into me.

How could I love something—anything—like this? What kind of a woman is she? How does she hold me? How did she find me? How in hell does this happen?

I have to see her.

It has been so long. It is one thing to sing about sirens and shores and danger, and something else entirely to hurt like this.

What am I thinking? I am in no state to be made any weaker than I am. It is time to put them, and her, out of my head; I will block the music and open another bottle—several bottles—of wine.

I sit very still for a very long time. There is nothing to break the silence I bring.

After a long, impossibly long time, more than I can stand, I come to understand that what heart I have is unquestionably not in my control. This definitely does not please me, but I cannot escape it.

This insane, wretched, altering love. How many ways can it hurt me? How many places do I find it? In my own landscapes, for heaven's sake.

Again, I wish I were not the gentleman I am, so I could give birth to an epic (actually) stream of invective and verbal linguistics that you would be lucky to hear. Your education has been tragically curtailed by my, as always, perfect manners.

Let it suffice to say that whatever the past may look like, you have no way of knowing for certain what it was, what has actually happened, anywhere. Enjoy the sensation.

Would you like to be even more confused?

I have aroused your curiosity; I can tell.

Perhaps I will tell you about her—the other her.

Well might you groan and roll your eyes incredulously, someone else, something else? I know exactly how you feel. She is—trust me—something else entirely.

There was a song.

That is where I broke in, the witless, undeserving wretch that I was, momentarily, only at that point, when she was almost dead.

It doesn't matter. What matters is that she did not die. Perhaps we could talk about something relevant.

Look, I did not have to tell you anything about her—it. Technically, I am not telling you anything useful—or important, for that matter.

I do not even know why I am telling you. It is a hard one to tell. But you will no doubt hear it from somewhere; I may as well give you the true version.

Or you could ask her.

I would imagine she has splashed it out into the universe in her wanton, abandoned way. No doubt if you look for it, you will find it.

This is the story in short form; my time is valuable despite the endless supply. At any rate, I do not wish to waste it on this repetition of my very minor transgression.

I think we will find that once I have told you about her, you will see that it is all largely her fault since she is quite literally insane. Furthermore, evidence will show that she lured me—quite perfectly, actually—and conditions were, as you may remember, not ideal for me personally but certainly ideal for something.

Let me tell you about her. How many times have I had to write that sentence in the last—whatever minute amount of time I have known Aela, which is where everything went to hell. Not the best time to think of her.

Let us see if I cannot.

Loneliness—not a word ever associated with myself. It can make you do things you would never otherwise think of—well, that and pure, insane, powerful pain. Godlike pain. You cannot even conceive of it; do not try.

That is where I was at the time. You may recall some of the attempts I made to surround myself with something.

You may also recall that I had wreaked a somewhat unusual amount of havoc, let us say, in your world. At various times and places, there was a great deal of smoke and blood. I forget the details; things were burned, and others were frozen.

This, in turn, created ripples that spread outward. Things were not pleasant; it was cold, all the fires could not warm you, so you grew desperate, as often happens.

Sacrifices—for some reason, you always sacrifice things. Like we want you to kill things and splash their blood around. Ridiculous, really, entirely our prerogative, so how could it please us when you do it? To each other, yes, but the whole idea of sacrifices, willing or otherwise, is so overdone.

Every age, every kind of people—all of you sacrifice things. Smart ones use it to get rid of their enemies or manipulate others. We enjoy that sort of thing, but it has to be done very well to amuse us; we have seen the best.

The most boring, tedious ones are the self-sacrificers, the martyrs. They do it to please whatever god they make up in certain places—what a tremendous waste of energy and sometimes even creativity. (Although we recruit, obviously.) For a while, I did find them mildly amusing, but they are not even good target practice since they stand still.

But religions, while excellently convenient for our purposes, are tremendously, exhaustingly boring. Of all the things that bore me (and there are many—I have lived, well, forever), I think religions, in any manifestation, are the very worst. I do not hate them—*hate* is a word I use judiciously and only where deserved—but they bore me quite painfully.

So I rarely pay any attention to them. She might not have known this about me, but either way, that was a significant risk she took. She is brave.

If it hadn't been for her song—it was quite a close thing.

She is striking, astonishingly animated, and lovely. Like a small, vibrant female version of, just a tiny bit mind you, but she does have the whitest skin and the blackest hair. Odds are good that someone would have drawn my attention to her, as soon as she caught someone's attention, that would have happened without doubt. Eventually.

It could have been too late, though. So you can be sure that someone will be dealt with.

The song was remarkably forward and well informed. I cannot think how she could know half of what she knows, but she does. She sang it out into the cold black air of the winter around her as she lay there dying, bleeding out onto the pitiless stone beneath her under my pitiless sky. I barely heard the last few lines; I had to go personally. I carried her like the fragile, impossible, almost-dead, priceless creature she was. I laid her in a bed of the softest, warmest east winds, in my arms like a goddess.

Then I gave the priests and the people—the stupid, wretched, pitiful creatures that could willingly take a life like hers on any pretext—all the warmth they asked for. More heat than they would ever have used if they had lived.

Their altar I flung into the night sky as hard as I could, and it will take a few more useless lives when it lands.

I have no idea how she even came there, more than a thousand years from where she was born.

She brings "Vokuro" to show me that she can be found in many places and at many times, in any time.) She has the voice of stories, the kind of enchanting, eternal, exquisite voice most commonly found, well, you know where, and she wanted to find her way here.

She was incensed that I had not found and taken her, as I should have—as I did.

(I still have the marks on my back from her injured pride.)

I cannot think how such a thing happened—any of it, but specifically the music. I could not fail to hear her now that I have heard her. I think we can guess who else can hear her. Every one of them will, without doubt.

I imagine they are clamoring like wolves and hammering on the doors somewhere. What a tremendous headache she is. I do not have the energy for someone like her *and* Aela.

But she was so close, even then, to here, and I had never heard her. It makes me quite sick to think of it. It is likely my own fault somehow, but I will blame that too on others.

She is not Aela. Nothing could ever be anything like Aela. God, I miss her. I was missing her. I have missed her every second since I met her, even when I was with her. She drives me crazy, so crazy.

There, now I will be happy to talk about anything you like so long as it is not Aela. What would you like to know? I can certainly guess, as any idiot could.

Let me tell you about her then—tell you the rest of someone who probably is, actually, mad. She is a crazy, (coincidence?) chameleon-phoenix-hawk-seductress-suppliant-impudently equal mortal. One of the strangest thing I have ever encountered, besides Aela.

What do I call her? A woman? Girl? Sprite? Seductress? Demi-Muse? (She would be the first, but I think it would be an excellent concept. Perhaps I will implement it; even sylphs and nymphs and sorcerers like to be stroked.) Names are leaping into my mind; I will try to stay focused. I go on. Insidious nemesis? Dangerous goods? Sex personified? Witch? I assure you she is all those things and many more. I do not know what to make of her.

She brings "Wanderlust" and confuses me again. I am tired of lessons.

She was ready to die in a strange place and time, far from any who might try to stop her. Anyone who cared. And to your kind, it looked as if she were willing to give up her life to placate me or others like me. Ordinarily, tremendously futile, but occasionally, it serves our interests to make use of those impulses that arise so marvelously easily in you.

She has said she wanted to be here, or where she believes the music is, and so she should be. I have no argument, but still, it does not sit right, not entirely. It is a plausible enough story. She is obviously a strong, wide-open channel, and she should have every resource available to harvest the results.

All of this makes simple sense but does not explain how she knew what was, without doubt, part of her song— Aela and I. What we were, what we are, and some vague, naive ideas about ways to make things better. I missed most of it, and I do not need to hear it.

I should not be surprised at anything by this point, but I can be puzzled, and I am.

In truth, it roused more anger than was likely intended; she does not know me well enough to understand how much of a bad idea it is to pass comment on my actions. But she knows enough to know that I never shy from the truth, and this gets my attention. Again, I see that she is very well informed. What a puzzle she is. What a proper minx.

I can only imagine all the kinds of hell she will raise when I do one day escort her into the music halls.

This brings me back to Aela again. I tell you, you will never hear what you are interested in hearing this way.

It is clear I have not consumed sufficient quantities of things to share indiscretions. I rectify this as quickly as the laws of physics allow. (What physical laws did you think I would follow? But that one is not under my control, or it would have been modified by now.)

But understand that it must be a very specific, quiet kind of known. It is a safety issue, quite crucial, and if it were ever compromised, I could certainly not be responsible for the consequences, nor could I entirely control them. There is every possibility that I would be subject to forces outside of my control, and everything else would be at the mercy of something far worse than I could ever, ever be.

(She brings "Joga" now, and this pleases me regardless. Listen. It is breathtaking; you might even understand.)

Fine. I will tell you, but I would like the proper background. I suggest you listen, as I am now writing this, to "Pagan Poetry." From this point on, I will likely begin to lose control.

This is what happens then. I hear her and all the insane, magical ways she has made to surround us with other her.

And then I listen to what she is saying.

I can hear it with everything I have, which you do not. No one does, except Aela.

And her.

I go and find her.

I am feeling her as I look for her. I am with her, in her, lost in her. She is dancing, all over my body, with her voice, and her words. It is like a – some kind of cool, healing liquid, like soft and forgiveness, and warmth and lust and desire and, somehow, every woman that ever lived, even Aela, in there somewhere, lost in the wild world of color that she is apparently made of.

When I find her, she is everything I knew she would be— and so much I could not have imagined. She is so physical.

I lose track of my narrative. I am stopped now for I do not care how long while I listen—and feel.

I press repeat.

Listen, and you will hear what I could not help doing to her, to her white skin, exactly like mine but warm. And the rest of her, never still— a flame I cannot pin down. She is many things I have never encountered. But I am not in her, and she is not in me. She is with me; we are together here in her room, in my world. For a long, *very* long time I am inside her. She is everywhere, like a full fire, dancing and hot and confusing.

I can tell you that I found her astonishingly different. From everything I have seen, and from Aela, and from things I have fashioned. I will tell you that nothing remained untasted, nothing unfelt.

It was intensely erotic; it weakens something in me to remember it even. It was very much pagan poetry.

I know. I have heard it through the centuries; it was chanted for me. When it was good, I listened; it raised the hairs on my neck the way she does.

It was wild enough to make me dizzy.

My skin remembers; it hurts.

She is not Aela. I do not know what to do about her. I am perhaps the very slightest bit worried about the kind of complication she could potentially be. The kind she has already been.

And at the end, you may hear how I left her.

I will not tell you how it felt to leave her or how I have felt since.

I have no idea what to do with her. She is far too volatile to be safely put anywhere she does not want to be, or where she does. Who knows what she might do? With her music, her voice, her beautiful, mysterious mind that I cannot see into. She is as fascinating as she could be without being Aela.

I let her into music halls once, just for a moment. That was all it took. She found her way to Wistan, and God knows what else she did while she was loose, with my beautiful, trusting, vulnerable Aela. My Aela. And him, and him, and the rest of them. What a glorious mess this could be if I were inflicting it instead of enduring it.

I am not enjoying this, being tangled in webs that are not mine and suffering consequences.

Since this is not a state I am willing to grow accustomed to, I have mastered the situation. For the time being, she is remaining as my honored, somewhat reluctant guest. She can make all the music she wants to; anything and everything is at her disposal.

She breaks my heart with it more than I can stand at times. But I have no idea what else to do. I cannot think straight.

Before you rise too hard against me, remember what you have learned about me, that things are not always in my control. That what I inflict I also endure. That for every lethal blow you will hear when you listen, remember that I receive them also. And they can only be worse for me. It is well that I can take them.

Know that there are forces that someone like her can rouse—forces that will fly out of my control, and god knows how dangerous that is.

Do you not understand? Are you insane? Do you not care what is awoken?

Fine, stupid, unimaginative, close-to-dead you need me to feed you like a baby.

From the beginning.

I am an immortal god whose job it is to perpetually raise hell, in short, and who was somehow invaded by a combination, bunch, whatever you want to call it, (*still happening right now*). Kind of distracting, being invaded by a rabble of impossible things in impossible ways, while struggling manfully to fulfill my 'duties,' the consequences of which can be unfortunate, admittedly.

I still have to do my job. You have no idea what would happen if I did not.

I have already told you this. I am losing patience. I do not justify myself to anyone—well, except Aela.

So, as I have mentioned before, when I suffer, everything suffers.

And fearful men make desperate promises; they look for places to lay blame, gods to appease, all the sorts of things that need victims. There must always be a victim, and the gold standard in victims, as far as men are concerned, is a willing one.

They will find new ways to make them. You will always rise to every opportunity to hurt your own. Did I condition you for it? Did I make this in you?

You flatter me. I have neither the time nor the patience. A world like yours requires a combination of wildly varied, unique qualities, all present at roughly the same time, overlapping sometimes and often unpredictably. With enough interesting anomalies to keep us stimulated.

(See much of the ancient world, the aforementioned 'renaissance', the 'Elizabethans', parts of the twentieth century, Iceland, Asia, and my personal 'catalogues' for a few stellar examples.)

It needs a generously numb, mindless, acquiescent, utterly unscrupulous, and pathetically weak collection of humanity willing to sell their own soul for a promise.

That is where you come in. *(Thank goodness for you. How else would my staff get their well-earned vacations?)*

Do you find this harsh? I believe it based on what I have seen, but I invite you to prove me wrong.

I need to see Aela. I cannot see her, but I need so very badly to see her and smell her and feel her.

Sometimes I dream. I imagine I could just open my mind to her. Just that. Nothing else.

I am afraid I will lose my mind without her.

I am afraid of what that would mean. What would happen.

If I lost my mind.

Consider it like this: I have had to make space for Aela. Huge, tremendous amounts of space she takes up. And for the rest of them, they have made plain that they will never leave, as much as some of them might want to. I can assume all the space they occupy is gone. In my domain but no longer within my sovereignty. Ridiculously dangerous.

Ah! You have no idea how angry and desperate it makes me.

I hope you see that we are all equally helpless.

I do not know myself. Who said that?

I answer, "As much as equal can mean between a god and all of you."

I will see her. Nothing could stop me. I just have to find a way that is safer.

I use what I know and what I remember, and I use them.

They know how it was. They know it, they saw it, they wrote it, and they sang it while it burned around them. It was a long time before they could get the scent out of their hair.

They were there. They saw her gripping her basket tighter and walking faster to reach the safety of her pitiful hut, as if she could stop what was coming. She knew—and they knew—there was nothing she could do. No law or higher power to appeal to, no benign, invisible force working strings that could save her. No hero to ride into this nightmare and take her away, far away from the kind of evil that lived in this village, that lives in every village.

That is one way I punished all of them, although I prefer to call it broadening their education. Always a noble endeavor, yes? I made them see in every way they can, so many more ways than normal, sane other men. I made them see and feel and hear and wear it in their skin permanently. They have their own unique senses, you might say. I know how and where to teach them.

I did not hurt them. I just made them watch.

But it is not all bad. Am I a monster? One day it will make them wealthy.

I listen. I learn the other sides. I listen to their song, so perfect, so eloquent. I imagine the fire from a more personal place.

(Later, I learn that he sang for her, playing his own guitar, under a tree, one of my trees. And the rest of them came; he sang "Give Up the Ghost." They wrapped it around her; they cannot help that. It is the way it works, even on me.)

And I understand—I have to understand—just the tiniest, infinitesimal fraction of a degree how something could happen after that.

(Do not wait for me to mention my own indiscretion. It was nothing like that kind of betrayal. You should be grateful I do not mention it.)

I call them here just for a fraction or even less.

I freeze and come to my senses.

I let them loose in the wind, in the black night that surrounds me, wherever I am.

I let them go where they want; they are kind, and they sing the same song for me as they leave: "Give Up the Ghost." It is so quietly meaningful, so more than I want anyone to know. When it is finished, he knows what I have understood, and I can see what he has somehow found out.

(Afterward, they leave me "The Gloaming." Listen to it if you want to know.)
(And when that makes you afraid, listen to "Spectre.")

I call Dorian to me and light a different kind of fire. It is time to look for Aela. I need to know.

You will have to wait to see what I see. What I have done. And what I do.

Chapter 24

AELA

I awake from a deep sleep, and I am walking, alone in the blackest night, through a silent forest. Fear floods through me, but I keep walking. I cannot stop. My arms hang limply at my sides. I could not raise them if I tried, but my legs walk on. Through soft velvet grasses that I cannot see; they are black like everything else around me. But they are so soft.

I know there are trees all around me; they are their own kind of black. Their branches caress my face and comb the tangles from my hair with gentle fingers. This is the most unknown forest, dense and black but so very safe for me. It is a woman's forest; the trees are entwined, but they let me pass through them, and what fear I had is brushed from my skin.

This must be a dream. I struggle to remember where I am and where I was before the forest took me. There is a glimpse of light. It flashes briefly in my mind before it is gone, and I realize that my mind itself is also black. Eyes open or shut, thinking or not, I see nothing, just the trees. This makes me stop.

I stand completely still; I kill what senses are still in my control to some degree. I focus on that brief flash of light. What was it? What did I see?

Nothing distinct but enough to remember fire; warmth; and a face I am a slave to, that I love and fear and loathe. And desperately, desperately need.

It fades, and I am left with the noble darkness of the woods around me lending me strength. and I close my eyes and start to walk again. My arms lift themselves up and out; my fingers tremble through leaves that whisper into my skin.

135

From the deep black silence I hear the faintest music. It is being pulled from the earth by the roots of the trees and singing up through the swaying trunks into the branches.

When the leaves begin to sing with a woman's voice, I recognize it immediately. It is a voice I have heard since I took my first breath. It is at once familiar and mysterious. She is singing now in the most exquisite, personal way. It lights shivers on my soul. She is using my words—my own carefully chosen, painfully assembled words—strung together in my crude, halting, pitiful manner. She has transformed them into the most heartbreakingly beautiful language. She is singing my pain; she is singing Pandor for me, from me, and into me.

Who is she? How can she know?

The woods come to an end. There is a black lake shining and sleek under the starlight, full of promise. It calls to me, and as I walk into its inky depths, it feels even softer than the forest I have left behind. The soft warmth welcomes me like a child into a womb.

I am not afraid; I will not drown in this lake of black potion.

I do not float; instead, I walk down the gentle slope to the very bottom. Some small part of me, like a spark somewhere, thinks of breath and wants to panic, but I do not. I sink slowly into the warm arms of the ground beneath me, and the view changes. Upside down, it makes a bowl of black water lit by stars behind it. In it, I see myself.

The lovely voice has followed me down; it resonates through the water around me, trying to comfort me. She has brought, like magic, the pain in my life. A reflection somehow of the pain in hers.

It unfolds before me, and I have to watch while someone who looks like me suffers the kind of things no woman should ever know. She is tossed about in terrible, hostile winds and tortured in the most subtle, evil ways. All her blessings are shown to be curses of the vilest sort.

When she turns and tries to bite back, I am not surprised, but I did not really expect her to win. I hate her. I hate her for her weakness, and her just taking it, and endlessly trying to be good. I hate her for failing.

I curse her myself.

The voice has stopped now. Instead, I hear what I have learned are called violins—lots of them—wailing into the sky above the lake and calling out into the stars. And she comes like something I have learned is a rocket, a living star blazing through the night straight to the black heart of this black lake.

Like lightning drawn to water. The flash blinds me; the light explodes like fireworks around me, and I am seared and stung by bits of light. Before I can scream, it is gone. The pain, the light, the vast aching hole in my heart where the worst things I have done lived. Everything is gone.

She carries me lightly and easily in her arms out of the water. I am warm. I am understood. I am forgiven. I sleep.

Chapter 25

I open my eyes. Dawn is long past; it is safe. The walls are my own, wooden and hung with tapestries, given to me by generous, welcoming women. Wives, witches, and others I have never met. I am in my bed under layers of fur; the shutters are closed, but the light and smoke from an outside fire somewhere find their way in.

I remember now. I remember many things I had forgotten and much I could wish had remained forgotten, but it does not hurt me now, so much. I could thank the dream if I did not know for certain that it was not.

I sit up and find the new, delicate chain that hangs between my breasts, with its tiny glass phial twined in silver scrolls. I hold it to the firelight that flickers, untended and eternal, on my own hearth. The liquid lets in no light; it could not be blacker, and it sends a shiver down my spine. This is not water I have ever seen, but I do not have to open it to know that it is clean black water and that it will heal. It is a priceless gift.

What I do not know is the how of it. I wash and dress, carefully winding linen beneath my tunic to keep the phial safe against my skin. I need answers, and I know where to find them.

I wrap a cloak around my shoulders and begin to lace up my boots, and something makes me stop. I freeze and listen, and though I hear only the snap of the fire, I know there is something outside my door. I could swear it; I jump up and open it as fast as I can, all in one motion.

He is lying across the threshold. He lifts his head and thumps his tail, and I drop to the ground and bury my face in his fur. I do not care how he is here, one more question in a long list. My heart is overwhelmed. What it must have cost him to find my dog that was not always my dog. Now, at this particular time.

How can I ever understand a man like that? A god like that?

I try not to think about everything else that comes with this precious, so, so welcome friend. I push it all out of my mind for the time being.

I rub vigorously behind his ears, then hold his head still; look into his wonderful, intelligent eyes; and ask him, "Are you hungry, my friend?" He thumps his tail again, I hug his ribs, and we get up and go through the woods to find the fire, the food, and the answers.

Wistan rises to greet us with meat and drink; Gunn rubs his face into his tunic, lingering a little with his kindred spirit. I meet Wistan's eyes briefly, noting that he shows no surprise at seeing my new guardian.

I pass beyond him, the blood draining from my face, I can feel it, because across the fire, I see her. I think. Tiny black and white and sparks and something fey. Something at once newborn and ancient, a face that never looks the same twice and is impossible to pin or describe, and sure enough, she is gone.

What was that, a fraction of a second? I cannot help myself. "Wait! Please!" I cry to the space she left behind. I twist around. "Wistan! Who was she? Where did she go? I need to know her! I do know her; I know her voice."

I stop. I think of the lake and the phial between my breasts that keeps its own warmth and secrets. I have no idea what was real or not, how it was contrived, or why it even happened. I am not clear myself on what has happened. Far too many things for me to process, let alone understand.

All I know for certain is that I must always reveal little and question much. I must always do the asking and only be answerable when I have no other option. I know this in my bones; the knowledge was put there by someone I trust, and everything I have experienced since then has only served to confirm it.

So, I turn back to Wistan, smiling; shake my head; and hold out my hands for a bowl and a cup. I am famished, but before I hand control of myself to a wineskin and a circle of unscrupulous bards, I look them all in the eye. One by one, I let them see my determination, my will.

I have been all but absent for the longest time, mired in misery and ruled by blind anger.

I ranted, I screamed to the skies and hoped to deafen him. Deafen all of them, playing games with souls, recklessly and carelessly.

And when I was exhausted, and I could no longer rave and fight and block them out, I was helpless, and so I listened helplessly, while they changed the world around me and made it theirs.

Slowly, they crept into my heart and then my soul, twining like young vines, quietly and gently taking over—all of them.

Thinking of it makes me shudder and yearn at the same time.

I have abandoned reason and embraced madness; I have been ravished by creative life. I have been its willing slave; I have been their willing slave. I will never be entirely free of them, any of them or all of them.

They have come to me. I remain, in some ways, powerless beneath them, within them, of them. I have given myself to them in many ways.

He can blame himself for this.

He left me here with them—locked in, surrounded by obedient winds and blind accomplices, at the mercy of words and light and sound and minds and souls— and bodies. Well, one body, but the consequences—I cannot think of them.

All who sit with me around this fire with their warm and open faces— they have watched. Some played their parts with true feeling and generous impulse; others with an eye to what it might gain them, but a story is a story, and to a man, they watched.

They are not slow, these friends of mine. They know a shipwreck when they see one.

I have been down. How could I be otherwise? I miss him so much.

How can he do this to me? How could he do what I am all too certain he has done?

I look at them carefully. I do have a story to tell them, one they will not have expected, and I will trade it for some of the things I need to know.

I have been down, yes, further than anyone will ever know, but this is no longer the case. For the moment, I have mastered my weaknesses, and they can spare themselves the trouble of trying to exploit them.

All of this I convey with my eyes. They are, singly and collectively, knocked onto their figurative backsides. They will find that I have learned far more than pretentious analogies and a mesmerizing gaze from our lord and master.

The bread is hot. I blow on it to cool it and dip it into warm honey. They are watching me patiently while I eat, so I take my time. They think that I will eat faster if they watch me, because few women like to be the only person eating, but I am not usually that kind of woman. I never was, but I have had hours of practice under the relentless, chilling—okay, smoldering—gaze of Pandor, who could not be taught manners to save his soul.

140

Thinking of him makes me lose my appetite, so I give the rest of the bread to Gunn and wipe my hands on the side of the nearest leather-clad leg.

I look at Wistan and nod toward Esla, who, as a scribe, always has ink and parchment with him. "Ask him to sharpen a quill and find a blank piece that he will not mind losing, please, my old friend." I smile enough promise at him to make him forget that this is my idea.

They are all astonished to find that I can write, and read, and work numbers. For genii, they are remarkably slow. I look at them and roll my eyes. Was it not the first thing each of them learned when given the least chance? And for most of them, the magic of numbers and music followed. Lucky them.

For me, it is enough that I can record the arrangement I want to make with them, and they will learn about other darker kinds of contracts.

I am sitting on a bench, the same simple wooden bench she was sitting on when I saw her for that brief flash. I have been enjoying its warmth while I eat and doing my best to discomfit the young man next to me. He is someone I do not know, the second stranger by this fire tonight.

In this world of limits, it is not an everyday occurrence.

Neither was I, so I know enough to be prepared and mildly alarmed. But Gunn is not, so I do not know what to think. I make a small diversion; it is best to use every opportunity to unsettle potential opponents. I intend to use all of those at my disposal.

I turn to the quite noticeably anxious face beside me and smile warmly. I hold his eyes while I put down my bowl and pick up the inkpot and paper. He looks down at them in my hand and stares as if they are wands or tokens of strange magic. He does not feel my other hand on his back until he is halfway down, and by then, it is too late. He is a desktop, and his dignity is none of my concern.

It will teach him to be wary of sitting next to unpredictable women. He will be properly primed for when I question him later—and I intend to question him.

I raise my face and turn to Wistan.

"I know what you want, all of you. I will tell you, but you should know that you will pay well for it and that you cannot have it first."

I stop there to let them wonder. The silence grows, broken only by the snap of fire and the hiss of hidden things burning. I wait. For something.

Do not ask me how I know it. I have no memory of it, but it must be so, since we all begin to hear it at the same time: her lovely, living self. I

141

can hear its heartbeat and feel its lifeblood coursing through the wonder of her voice and the wonder of her beautiful, mysterious words. Not one of us understands the language, but we all hear the story—my story.

I did not know I had told her, until I knew.

Hearing her now, watching her effect on a circle of still and spellbound listeners, I think of what she must endure, what she has endured, and I shiver.

She is, after all, one of them, and like all of them, she must know it to bring it to life for those who listen.

But it is different somehow when she brings it. I am not the only one who feels this and hears what is new. Everyone sits absolutely still, frozen into something that none of us wishes to break. It awakens a memory in me, in us, of something we all must have known sometime or somewhere in our varied lives.

I will tell you, it sounds like some kind of hope.

It is nonsense, of course, but the idea is enough to hold anyone. Even those of us who have been involved with the smooth-talking, mercurial, infuriating mess that is Pandor. We who should know better. Certainly it has never been seen or felt here. It has been imagined, but felt?

She makes no reference to it; her words, understood or not, are those of a victim, a survivor of something. We do not need to know what to appreciate all that it implies.

Hope is a lovely, naive concept easily embraced by those who have no idea.

A promise, a whisper only the truly desperate can hear, the particular domain of charlatans and tricksters in every age. It has no business here, in her. Whoever she is.

It is indescribably lovely and ephemeral. I let her end it how she likes. Silence falls and is filled once again by the fire.

We are all lost in its depths, but we see it now; we understand how it could not be a refuge in a very dark place. They see it.

When I raise my eyes to Wistan's, his are melting and gentle, though he does not know the half of it.

Beneath my arms, I feel the corded, tensely wound strength of angry muscles. He is breathing hard and clutching my skirts. I lift my arms and lean back to let him sit up. His flushed face and tousled hair stop in front of mine. His hands follow and cradle my face, an ageless, quiet pity warring with the hero in his head. He is too late to save me. He is so young.

I look down at the parchment clenched in my hand as if it could mean something.

I put it down on the bench and brush my skirts slowly. A dozen pairs of eyes follow my hands, looking for traces, as if it should show.

"Do not ask me questions I could not answer if I wanted to. But if you want to know how it felt—"

Others come walking out of the dark woods silently. Appearing by the fire and finding places that were never there but are waiting for them. The music starts to rise like unseen mist from the air around us, it sounds so friendly at first.

The same fatal sounds play hell on the small hairs at the back of my neck; it is a song I know.

It poisons me, the evil they understand so well. Like the slow breath of true darkness rising around us. I am not sure if I can take it. My throat is tight. I am not ready to see or hear him so soon. His voice wraps itself around me; it soaks into my skin and makes me weak. If I had known this was the price I would pay, hearing this and seeing him at the same time. And the rest of them. After her and so soon. And missing Pandor the way I miss him. I miss him so much. It all just overwhelms me.

Chapter 26

Pounding at the door. I sit up. I start to hear voices, low and mumbled at first, but they get louder and louder. My heart thrums in my chest. Where am I? Where is this? What is pounding on the door?

I am frozen in my bed. Through the shutter cracks I see torchlight—enough to form stark lines on the floor that move like a threatening sea between me and the door. They are screaming so loudly now outside. The pounding turns to blows, slamming on the door. The walls are fighting, but they will lose.

Nothing good can come through that door like this. I find my knives, a jug, and my talisman. Leave the wands hidden, no reason to inflame them. I tie my hair back quickly and firmly and stand facing the door. *Not without a fight. Not for them.*

They are growing reckless now; each lights the other. I have seen this before—a massive fire that held the shades of many and silent screams that were too loud to bear. That deafened all my senses.

They are wide awake and working now. My heart pounds out its strength, ready for the battle. The door splits in its frame, pieces fly through the air, and they fall in.

They push themselves into the hut, shouting and cursing and mad to be inside. So many of them—faces I know, with strangers in their eyes. I look straight into them. They turn away. *Cowards.* I spit on the earth between us. The magic circle of firelight that embraces me but shuns them. They stop beyond its edge, feeling safe there.

Safe from me?

The noise has died down. Through the torches and heads, I see beyond the doorway. The forest around is lit with the same unholy torchlight giving its blessing to this night's work: Burn the Witch.

And I am the witch. Standing here with a knife in each hand, a scrap of fabric in my waistband. Deaf from the drumming of my own heart. I am strong, but I am terrified. I want to wake up now.

Suddenly, the flock is hushed, all silent at once, and moving to clear the way for a figure coming through. A tall, important man comes in to me with a hood hiding his face and shoulders bent with sorrow. There is no anger in him, nor is there in me, even after he lowers the hood and I see that he is my father.

I face him squarely, feeling so sick, so sad, and so betrayed. I hear his voice telling this insane mass of people that I am not his daughter if I am a witch. He turns and walks away, and then I scream at him, "On whose word? What proof, my father? Why in God's name? Why? You know I am no witch!"

I whirl to my left and slash out with my knife at the men who try to take me. They jump back. Two are bleeding, and that is a mistake. The sight and scent of blood attract every living thing; they all come at once, and then I fight furiously. With all my strength, I stab out at these enemies, even those who were my friends.

Other enemies come and do their damage. Time slows, so I can see those I cut, and I can see whose arms are bravest and strongest. Within the screams, the curses become specific; the voices become personal. I am accused of many things I could not possibly do and some I could if I chose to.

A bard, a smith, groomsmen, and warriors whose wounds I have tended. Who *lived*. God in heaven, the world has gone mad. Where is Gytha?

It is only a matter of time before I am forced to the ground, knives wrenched from my hands, hands crossed behind my back and tied so tightly I cannot feel them.

I go very still, letting my limbs go limp. They all jump back. What kind of fear is this? I roll to my side and look at them with the darkest eyes I can make, not a word. Something to really be afraid of.

I understand why witches in every age and in every case curse the people. Curse the blank, numb, bought evil of the people. Any fool can rouse it; the clever ones command it.

I look them in the eye and curse them one by one individually with things I would never wish upon them if they had only left me alone. And they *believe* me. I see new terror being born over and over again like an endless spring.

145

I understand why they have come to burn me. I do not care now. They have made me into this; I curse them with all the skills at my command.

Many begin to back away and melt into the night. Cross themselves and pray it is not too late to be turning around. Enough are left to take care of business.

A farmer's huge, rotting hands rip my braid free, and he winds it around his wrist, and I am dragged, like a runaway slave through the streets to the square. I stumble and run and ignore the filth that is thrown at me like an offering.

All around me, men and women reel back and detach themselves from me, denying me my mortal, normal human existence. Making of me an other.

Making me something they can terrorize, torture, and freely hate for any reason. Something with no rights. This I am afraid of—this and the fire.

I am lucky. The less courageous have occupied themselves in the square, building the fire for me. It burns high and hot already, so at least it will not be a long, drawn-out thing at the end.

I feel its massive heat from the moment I enter the square. It lights the faces, dances with steel, and glints on prayer breads. The worst kind of light. It illuminates the lies only and turns them into sacred truth, the dogma of death.

It makes heretics wherever it wants to. For the sheer joy of punishing something.

An implacable enemy, it wears many faces, and you can find traces of it in places you could never imagine.

I cannot help but see it in the circle of the fire. Hemwyth is there with his arms around Gytha, shielding her from the sight of me. His face is turned away, but I can see his closed eyes and his wet ravaged face. I stop and stand firm. They cannot force me to move if they tear my hair from its roots.

Everything around us goes silent, and I stare at Hemwyth's face. They will not burn this witch until I see it in his eyes, whatever it is that lets him be standing there that way, on the other side.

I will find it. I will find out.

I call all my strength, rip my hands free from the ropes, rip my hair from hostile hands, and run. As fast as I can, straight into the fire. No screaming. The blood from my wrists runs through my fingers as I pull

146

the fabric from my waist. I am blinded, fighting hot white winds and pain I have no words for.

I draw in my breath and throw the scrap into the air above me. The dust gets sucked into the flames, the flames turn black, and then I scream.

Chapter 27

I scream to reach the ends of all worlds. And I do. When I open my eyes, I am damp and shivering in his arms, in my bed under the tree.

The room is dark, lit only by the white flames in the black wall. The flames are dancing wildly in the grip of unseen winds. I have never seen them like this.

He pulls away from me and searches my face. He sees the shadows move on my skin, and the flames flutter into stillness, dimming their light and growing soft. His hands talk to me through my skin, soothing everything he can reach. His voice finds and takes care of the rest of me.

It was a dream—a nightmare. For now, I am happy to believe it. He leans back onto the headboard, and I drape myself across him. I forget the rest. God, it is him, alive and cold-hot beneath my hands. I cannot hold on hard enough.

I do not have to work to focus all my attention on him—all my relief, all my dizzy. How he smells, how his flesh becomes anything I need it to be. I find it with my hands, my tongue, my body. He plays with me. No one is keeping track.

But things get wild; storms sweep through. Snow, frost, searing heat, and insane, uncontrollable lust.

I give everything I have—almost. All the women I am come, and we surround him. We do whatever it takes to push him over the edge. He can only resist one at a time.

When he opens his eyes, he is damp and shivering in my arms. I run my fingers through his hair; it curls itself around my hands. I feel his skin, a part of mine. It almost works.

It is his skin that does it—his beautiful, perfect skin, with all its changing temperatures and messages. The skin of a god. What would fire do to skin like that? I shudder and sit up, pushing him off me.

Not nearly as easy as it sounds.

He rolls onto his back and puts his arm over his eyes. "For a woman whose mind I can enter, you are insanely unpredictable, Aela."

I come very close to actually snorting. "Oh please!" is out before I can stop it. I close my eyes and count. When I open my eyes and look at him, he is looking at my breasts as if they are the only things in the room. I cover up.

"Tell me how these candles work, my lord. Why do I feel as if I know them? And what are the black flames? How are they lit? Why are they not hot? Why are there so many different kinds of fire? Why is nothing ever what it seems with you?

"What exactly has happened? Anywhere, everywhere, in whatever, in all of the times?" *Please let me borrow from your modern friends. I am beyond caring about words. Or memories—any of it.* "What the fuck is going on?" *Oh my God, it feels marvelous to say it. It is perfect.*

"How is it all connected? I know it all connects with your work; we can call it that. I need to know how it is done. I am entitled to know. I am asking you to put your own interests aside. Can you even? Put them aside, and be the gentleman I know you are. Of course you are! Could you doubt it?"

I sit back on my heels, actively looking for patience, willing him to forget, willing myself to forget. Pulling everything away from our picture that is not naked truth. It stands there starkly, a very bleak picture. A journey cut short by means of some kind of magic. At the end of the road, the magician, lighting all the fires, drawing all the swords, hurting things but keeping his hands clean. Playing with the dice of death, as if it could be a game.

There is no place in me for something like that. But when he holds out his hands, I go.

PANDOR

"I will not deny it, that was 'quite a mindful,' Aela, my woman of words. Even for you."

At this point, I may, in some slight, trifling manner, call upon certain resources and let them say things for me. I would be a fool to call anything but "Spectre." And I think we have established that I am far from it. I make them come, and they play as if their souls depend upon it.

She sees right through that, of course, but she is still powerless once it starts, as I am. Only I am not quite, since I called for it, and I am prepared.

"Forget the candles, forget nightmares, forget my work. I am so tired of my work. Aela, please, give me a chance to recuperate. Give yourself a chance to breathe and to feel things other than fear or pain."

I do not mention other things she has felt, things I was not a part of.

"Let go of what you need to know, what you have seen, and what has hurt you, my love. It is so simple a matter. There are reasons; they will speak for themselves. Come and listen again, my Aela. Listen to the voices calling."

I defy her to hear it now with me, with the scent of us lingering in the air around, and not understand. She will. She understands honor. It is— this is the simplest kind of honor, even if she cannot see it.

I coax her back into the whirling world, *not so easy this time*, crossing my fingers, whispering inane invocations, and doing my best to tilt the odds. Why not? I would be an idiot not to. It is, in fact, the sort of thing that might, in a working mind, be taken as a given. I would betray my own world to keep her; there is nothing I would not do.

They bring "Weird Fishes (Arpeggio.)" Yes, the field is theirs.

Lovely. To not exploit them would be a crime against them and the universe. Why should they belong only to one place in time or space? So that those who live anywhere else will never hear them? Is that not a crime of the most inhumane, cruel kind? And by whose order? Not mine. It makes no sense.

"Ah, hear them now, Aela. How insanely gifted they are! The kinds of genius they are. And there are others. Everywhere, if you are alert and aware, you can find them. I am always looking and listening. Forgive me, but I cannot hear them and do anything else at the same time. There are a few like that; they just waltz off with my wits."

I stand there witless. "See, Aela? See how they play with me? How they torment me? Think of the combination for me of hearing them and seeing you. At the same time. Smelling you, feeling you. They know. They enjoy it when I suffer. They do not trouble to hide it. You cannot imagine what it does to me."

She shivers and shakes me. "I have no need to, I can see it myself. Pandor, I beg you; please get control of your—what? Self? Please stop before you draw attention."

"Forgive me Aela my love; I thought you understood that it is beyond me now. At any rate, this serves as the perfect evidence, if you wish, that I am not the sort of immortal you ever expected to meet in person. With our skin touching and our spirits conjoining themselves in the strange, mystical, messed-up way they do."

It is the end of the song now, and he is saying what lives in me but only has voice through him. To the very word.

"This is exactly what I have been trying to make you understand, my Aela. How very much of everything is really not in my control. I am not sure myself what I do or have done recently. Not since you came. My beautiful, frustrating, perfectly confusing, perfect woman."

I cannot explain anything.

"That is why I bring you here. I left you here before to keep you safe, but it is the best place at the moment to try to understand me, or as much of me as can be understood."

I bury my face in her hair, with no hope of understanding her, and she has no idea what I could do for her, about her, and because of her. I breathe as deep as I can until I am dizzy and flushed with her. Why can I not just freeze it all right here, standing still and motionless, forever? Until we are melded together; it would happen that way.

Let the music become the world around us.

I could make us trees that live forever or stars—no, nothing to do but watch. Rocks then, or winds that blow endlessly together.

Any other way than the way we have to be now would be so much better.

I look at them over her head. They can play whatever they want. I dare them.

Chapter 28

I confess, I have trouble keeping track of my own narrative at times. Should I be surprised to find that of all the limitless worlds I could find or create, I am lost in my own? Worlds that I made, some of them just so I could destroy them.

I am also, for the first time ever, what some of you may choose to call 'hungover.' A decrepit, weedy little word that is, nonetheless, the most succinct representation of the affliction. You may allow your mind to wonder naively how much wine I may have consumed to render myself in the present condition. One which is convincingly portrayed, and made bleedingly obvious, by the quality of this paragraph.

Remind yourself, also, what sort of selection in expletives I might have at my disposal and consider yourself quite fortunate.

Things have been quite busy, actually. A great deal has happened that I am entirely unable to account for, an admission that pains me more than you can know.

I am, alas, able to account for more than I would like, which pains me even worse.

You will remind me that I may have, perhaps, if you choose to look at it that limited way, in some fashion, well, incarcerated Aela, again. Really, there are other ways of considering the situation. You can figure them out for yourself, I am not here to spoon feed you...

I sigh and roll my eyes and remind you that we are never playing on the same field, and that I do not have to tell you anything. Do not ask me why I am.

Truly, her safety is the most important thing I have ever valued, the only real, perfect goal I have ever had. It goes far beyond what I feel for her. You, reading this, you have no idea of the depths I can feel.

Of what I feel for her.

I have already made my thoughts on immortality quite clear. Worlds away from yours— filled with questing heroes and mysterious encounters with gods. It is not nearly as romantic as you think; it could never be an asset, only a liability, of the most diabolical kind. Immortality, love— these are the true tortures of existence. Together they can fell a god.

When I say it is endlessly, fruitlessly learning to feel, endlessly wandering, eternally homeless in the worst of all ways, you will start to have an idea of it. Add to it lessons repeated in perpetuity that you will never learn from, add boundless ability to loathe yourself and everything around you.

Where I have lived eternally, immortally, is somewhere you would never, ever want to live. It never changes. Endless versions of the same endless sameness.

But something has changed. And how can you blame me for needing to keep it safe? Keep her safe. So yes, she is hidden, let us say. In the only place I could think of.

I have thought of nothing else since.

I shake my own head. Some of it clears. What else can I think about? I will change the music.

I am again, for the first time, confused. Worse, uncertain, unsure, undone. Utterly. And likely other 'uns' as well. Unhappy.

Epically unhappy.

So, I go and find her, unseen, quietly, just to watch her.

With mixed results.

Once, a strange song came to me, like they do, finding me and making me listen.

The kind of earthy, ethereal juxtaposition that attracts certain kinds, that terms like 'Siren Songs' are made for, and things just happened.

That is how it works with some gods. We hear, we feel, you sing. Unmistakable sounds coming from eternal, unmistakable strings ... We know when you are calling us and why.

This causes all kinds of trouble.

I remember what it felt like. I keep my eyes closed. It comes to me, and I let it carry me anew.

I can and do make it happen again, now.

Aela lies there, a lovely shape, curled under the blanket like an invitation. I know she is not, but I just cannot leave her alone.

I let myself in, just the slightest bit of music, keeping her aware but putting her to sleep.

I mean to keep it like that. I try to stay away—I really do—but there is no way I can. I slip like a spirit around her until she is in my arms, asleep. I stroke her hair. My hand betrays me.

And then I smell her. I smell the life in her—and the woman. How can I help it? What can I do? I am powerless. There is no saving me. I do not want to be saved from this different kind of hell.

Drawn like the dead, to her. Across the river. Irresistibly. Eternally.

Not normally something I would submit to.

But here you are.

How many kinds of powerlessness are there? Is she a punishment? And would it matter if she was, after all, something else?

That I could think such a thing.

I am tired of waiting for you. Bring yourself into your hands and feel me here beneath you.

She is soft; she smells like Eden. She yields like a gift. I feel her both on and under my skin. She is what a goddess should feel like. I fall.

And fall. And fall.

She stops me. She wakes me up, shaking me and slapping my face.

What are you doing? Fool—insane man. Do you really have no self-control? Stop it now and be who you are.

I freeze. Literally. Scared to move or breathe or think. Or feel.

Nothing that can be seen or heard, anywhere but here. How did I forget this? And keep forgetting? Walls of wind or not, they have their own access and their own rules.

I pull away from her, which is— so hard to do. I have to leave myself and make an artificial space between us. I will talk to her. I bring a chair to sit near her. I change the music, pulling from pain rather than pleasure, and soon enough, she feels the difference. I can remind her about dreams and fire, and others, and she will be horrified; and the distance between us will be born.

I add wood to the fire. She will shiver soon enough.

"I have told you many things about myself and my existence."

I try to remember what, exactly.

"I know that you have heard a great deal from your bards. They will have told you what they know, and it is the truth. For them. As far as they can know."

Ah, this is so difficult. How do I make her understand how this works? How I work, how and where I am?

"I must try to help you see the true nature of time."

A change of tactic and a very tall order.

"It has been hundreds of years since I last had to give this kind of meaning to my words. I am not sure I remember how. I never have to. What I mean is that whatever I will arises around me, out of my own mind. It requires no effort on my part. I have all the help I could wish for when I cannot finish a vision— or a deed."

I stop and adjust my something. I cough, I think, and then I try again.

"I have not spoken about myself this way for a very long time."

She keeps her dark, watching eyes intense and liquid, I lose my train of thought, she says, "I doubt that you ever have, not really. Ever. Please, no lying or twisting words. No tricks. If you are going to talk to me earnestly, you must be earnest. How else will I learn to trust you again?"

Name of a god, how do I keep away from this?

"Please, you must stop saying things like that. It will be best if you try not to talk at all, my woman of words." *For so many reasons, yes.*

I turn my chair to face away from her, but I keep her in sight. I leave the music the way it is; he is here, singing "E-Bow" and far more eloquent than I will ever be.

"Think of your life as a line. Let me draw one with your wands and string, straight and as long as I can make it. Let me carve it in the earth for you so you can see that it has a definite beginning and a definite end. We will say that this line represents the life of a man, or woman, not your life."

I use a sword (will it distract her?) to cut it from wall to wall, deep in the dirt, in a line beneath the string. I will her not to ask questions.

"How are my wands here? Gunn! Where is he now? Do you have all my things? I need my things, Pandor."

I pretend not to hear her, wrapping the string around the wands. Tying careful, complicated, intentionally convoluted knots at the ends. I put them down in the shadows and begin to talk about a man and a line.

"At this end, he is born. When he lives through his birth, his line is born, tied to those of his mother and father, and everything that will ever happen to him is already written on it. He cannot see it, but others can— well, certain powerful others can. They are the authors of his life. I am an author of his life, to a degree.

"This happens almost effortlessly for us. It must. There are far more of you; your numbers always grow. We could never devote our attention to all of you, so we devised other means. We diversified, you might say. And we shared. What? Oh, things like ammunition, advice, ability. Pleasure, but there was only the one kind."

155

I should not be surprised to find that this, too, was a lie.

"At any rate, there is no commiseration—no honor among thieves. We are, after all, a reprehensible lot. We loathe and hurt each other as much as anything else. We walk on a sea of hate, nothing but enemies in sight, as far as the farthest horizon. This is not to say that some of us are not gentlemen; you may have heard of my legendary courtesy."

"Some of us have felt it, too."

"Aela! You must not. Are you hearing me? And I am certain that your memory is not so short. Listen to me, the wheels we set in motion set others in turn, and it all works—like a living thing. Spreading itself like a virus. What? No, you will not have heard of it anywhere, and it is far too complex for me to explain it to you. Just imagine something that creeps along the ground like a flood or a miasma. But it never stops. On and on forever, and it takes almost no effort from us. From me. My work is good. Self-replicating and constantly improving. In all the ways that count."

I face her fully for a long moment. I need her to know that despite what I am saying it has not been so for me, really, for a very long time.

"It is true when I say I have not talked about myself for centuries. I have not talked for centuries."

She looks confused; she does not know what to feel. I imagine I look the same. Her face is warming; her eyes start to connect with mine. I shake my head. She must not.

"I cannot say whether my solitude is an indulgence on the part of those who made me—unlikely—or my own creation. I do not care how I am alone, so long as I am. But all of us were—are—manifestations of the same powerful, awful purpose. We serve the same unseen, unknown masters. So rather than waste time trying to destroy each other, we created new villains. We created new victims. We cast ourselves the way we liked, but none of us ever forgot what we really needed to be afraid of. So we banded together as one, against all of you, because of them."

Well, that solves that problem. I can make it even easier for her.

But she is Aela.

"Who are you afraid of? What are you—all of you, any of you— afraid of?"

Immediate change of subject required. Confusion always works.

"Often, we are playing the same song at the same time. It makes the beautiful so much more so— breathtakingly alive. And it makes the ugly desperately, relentlessly cruel. There must be both.

"Ugliness itself is cruel. Those who do not know otherwise like to say that, like beauty, ugliness is in the eye of the beholder. A lie, in fact, and one of the most convenient in a portfolio of many. The truth is that ugliness, like pain, is custom designed for every one of you. In some way or another, like all the rest. Always personal, intimate. You all suffer quite uniquely. But you know this, my beloved woman. You know this."

I watch her close her shutters one by one. Slowly and carefully shutting out my words. I can hardly breathe.

I think of all the ways we are connected. It horrifies me. It makes me stronger. I remember that this is, after all, what I am very, very good at.

"We have endless ways to play with you when we want to. I know many of them, but I can only operate through my own means and work within them. You know me. You like to give names to me. I thank you for this."

I let some of them flood into my face, and I am Loki. I am Eris. I am Chaos. I am Satan. I am Lucifer, whom she hates the most, though she does not know it.

I am the Eternal Vampire who really does live forever. I am the Eager Hangman.

She recoils. She is horrified. Perhaps, for a moment, even terrified. This is so much worse than I thought it could be. *God, no.*

I am willing to admit of the possibility that I have no idea what I am doing. I have no emergency, contingency plan. How could I?

The music changes. The room melts and swirls with indescribably hopeful music: "And They Have Escaped the Weight of Darkness." Impossibly, inexplicably. Quite different things flood into me.

"That I could ever be something that gave you pain, Aela, woman of my world."

My mind weeps with ways to never let it be so. I am consumed. I am terrified. The music sows its light into perfect shapes. The small hut disappears, bleeding in at the seams.

I lose track, sight? Of where we are.

I lose sight of where we are.

Music for Aela's Story

Certain scenes in the text were written to or inspired
by songs, some of them are mentioned by name.
They are listed below in chronological order.

1. Einaudi, Ludovico. "Burning." *In a Time Lapse.*
2. Einaudi, Ludovico. "Run." *In a Time Lapse.*
3. Eluvium. "All the Sails." *When I Live by the Garden and the Sea.*
4. Richter, Max. "Last Days." *Memoryhouse.*
5. Morris, Trevor, Einar Selvik, Steve Tavaglione, and Brian Kilgore. "Vikings Attack." *The Vikings II Original Motion Picture Soundtrack.*
6. Einaudi, Ludovico. "Devenire." *Devenire.*
7. Einaudi, Ludovico. "Svanire." *Devenire.*
8. Einaudi, Ludovico. "Andare." *Devenire.*
9. Einaudi, Ludovico. "Oltremare." *Devenire.*
10. Sigur Ros. "E-Bow."
11. Arnalds, Olafur, and Alice Sarah Ott. "Verses." *The Chopin Project.*
12. Morris, Trevor, Einard Selvik, Steve Tavaglione, Brian Kilgore. "Jarl Borg Attacks Kattegat." *The Vikings II.*
13. Einaudi, Ludovico. "The Days." *Echoes: The Einaudi Collection.*
14. Einaudi, Ludovico. "Two Sunsets." *Echoes: The Einaudi Collection.*
15. Einaudi, Ludovico. "Waterways." *In a Time Lapse.*
16. Arnalds, Olafur. "Happiness Does Not Wait." *Erased Tapes Collection V.*
17. Moderat. "Reminder." *III.*
18. Sigur Ros. "Ekki Mukk." *Valtari.*
19. Sigur Ros. "Hrafntinna." *Kveikur.*
20. Sigur Ros. "Svo Hiljot." *Takk.*
21. Mansell, Clint. "Death Is the Road to Awe." *The Fountain.*
22. Radiohead. "Ful Stop." *A Moon Shaped Pool.*
23. Radiohead. "Weird Fishes." *In Rainbows..*
24. Radiohead. "Blow Out." *Pablo Honey.*
25. Sigur Ros. "Glosoli." *Takk.*
26. Obel, Agnes. "Fuel to Fire." *Aventine.*
27. Obel, Agnes. "Dorian." *Aventine.*
28. Radiohead. "Codex." *The King of Limbs.*

M. Dumonceaux lives in the country near Cochrane, Alberta, Canada. When she is not writing, she enjoys walking in the woods or tending to her garden.

Printed in the United States
By Bookmasters